"Leeanne McNab meet Gabriel Mendoza."

"Hi," he said coolly.

"Hi," she replied.

"I'll leave you two to get acquainted," Polly said. "Maybe you can play cards or something. Gabriel, you be nice now. We don't want you running off the help."

"I only run off the flakes," he replied, never taking his gaze off Leeanne.

He was very thin, she noticed, and dressed in a heavy pair of corduroy jeans and a thick wool shirt. His hair was jet-black, his skin a warm honey color, and his eyes a rich, velvety chocolate-brown. But it wasn't the unusual darkness of his gaze that startled her, it was the way he looked at her. For a brief moment she had the funny feeling that he could see all the way to her soul. . . .

DON'T MISS THE FIRST EXCITING BOOK IN THE *DEAR DIARY* SERIES:

Dear Diary: Runaway by Cheryl Zach

P9-CLO-378

THE DEAR DIARY *SERIES*

REMEMBER ME

Cheryl Lanham

BERKLEY BOOKS, NEW YORK

REMEMBER ME

A Berkley Book / published by arrangement with the author

PRINTING HISTORY
Berkley edition / February 1996

ISBN: 0-425-15194-8

BERKLEY®
Berkley Books are published by The Berkley Publishing Group,
200 Madison Avenue, New York, New York 10016.
BERKLEY and the "B" design
are trademarks belonging to Berkley Publishing Corporation.

PRINTED IN THE UNITED STATES OF AMERICA

10 9 8 7 6 5 4 3 2

This book is dedicated to the memory of Nancy Henderson. Teacher, wife, mother, and friend: She will always be remembered for her warmth, humor, compassion, and love by all of those who were lucky enough to have known her.

Chapter
One

September 18

Dear Diary,

My life is over and I might as well be dead. They gave me three hundred hours, three hundred, can you believe it, of community service. It's not fair. Terrorists or murderers don't get that much . . . but that lousy judge, she hated me. She wouldn't even let me say a word! She just sat up there and glared over the top of those ugly horn-rimmed glasses. She said she was sick and tired of spoiled rich kids treating this community like it was their personal playground and she was going to make an example of me. Those were her exact words. God, you'd think I'd stolen the Constitution or the Liberty Bell instead of one pair of lousy earrings. I tried to tell her that it was all just a prank. That I'd planned on paying for the earrings. But she didn't want to hear it. On top of that, Mom and

Dad took away my driver's license. I can't use my car now. It just isn't fair. I've never stolen anything in my life and the one time I do, I get caught. I can't believe this is happening. My whole senior year down the tubes . . . it can't get much worse than that.

A shrill ring sliced through the air. Leeanne put her pen down and snatched up the phone before it could ring a second time. Considering the way her luck was running lately, if her parents remembered she even had a phone, they'd take that away too.

"Hi, how'd it go?" her best friend Jennifer asked.

"Horrible." Leeanne pushed a lock of blond hair out of her eyes. "The judge hated me. She wouldn't even listen to my side of the story."

"She?"

"Yeah. It was a woman. But she wasn't exactly soft and cuddly and filled to the brim with understanding and compassion." Leeanne sighed. Telling this part wasn't going to be easy. Jennifer might be her best friend, but Leeanne was fairly certain she'd be on the phone half the night telling everyone in school all the gory details. Next to shopping, Jen lived for gossip.

"Well," Jennifer prompted impatiently. "Tell me. What'd they do to you? Put you on probation?"

"I wish." Leeanne frowned. "They sentenced me to three hundred hours of community service."

"Community service?" she yelped. "But that's

crazy. This was your first offense . . . it was a joke. Give me a break, anyone who knows you knows you're not a thief."

"Try telling it to the judge." But Leeanne was grateful for her friend's vote of confidence. As she'd stood there in that courtroom this morning with that judge glaring down at her, she'd felt like a criminal. It was horrible. Absolutely the worst experience of her life.

"Gosh," Jennifer continued. "Three hundred hours! What a colossal drag. You might as well take the veil and enter a convent. What about cheerleading? What about the decorations committee for the homecoming game? What about your social life?"

"According to Juvenile Judge Myra Bowen, I don't need one." Leeanne felt tears welling up in her eyes. She took a deep breath, refusing to let Jennifer hear her cry. "And they're going to make sure I don't have one too."

"Oh, God, you poor thing," Jennifer said sympathetically. "This is your senior year. The one year in high school you can actually have a good time."

"Well, I won't be having any fun," Leeanne said, her tone bitter. "We met with the probation officer right after the hearing. It looks like I'm gonna spend my free time emptying bedpans, pushing wheelchairs, or helping old ladies find their dentures."

"Gross." Jennifer sniffed delicately. "But that's not too bad. I mean, it could have been worse."

"Really?" Leeanne said. "I don't see how. My

senior year is in the toilet. I'm going to spend every waking moment either slaving at homework or picking up after old people. My parents took my driver's license away too. Frankly, Jen, I don't think it *could* get much worse."

But Jennifer, as usual, always wanted the last word. "It's better than picking up trash off the side of the road," she said. "That's what Mindy Waller's brother had to do when he got arrested for drunk driving."

"But I didn't do anything nearly as bad as that," Leeanne protested. "Mindy's brother almost killed someone."

"True, but you did get caught. Try looking on the bright side, at least if you're working at Community Hospital, you might meet some cute interns."

Leeanne's anger died as quickly as it had come. There was no point in taking her feelings out on her friend. "No such luck. I got stuck with a nursing home. A place called Lavender House. I have to start tomorrow."

"Tomorrow," Jennifer wailed. "But you can't. You'll miss cheerleading practice and you know what that means. Miss Devoe says if you miss two practices, you're out. You already missed Monday's."

Leeanne bit her lip. She'd give anything to turn back the clock. She'd give anything to have a chance to relive those few, fateful moments at Stoward's Department Store. Why hadn't she told Pru and her idiot friends to take a hike instead of going along with their stupid, stupid idea? She hadn't been planning to steal those earrings. She'd fully intended to leave the money on the counter, but Silvia Hawkins had been watching her and she'd been too scared of Silvia's mouth to do anything but stick the jewelry in her pocket and walk out. And look what it had cost her. Her whole senior year, that's what.

"Leeanne, are you there?"

"I'm still here," she said. She cleared her throat. "I'm afraid I'll have to give up cheerleading. I won't have time."

"Can't your father help?" Jennifer continued doggedly. "He's a lawyer, isn't he?"

Leeanne almost laughed except it wasn't funny. She didn't think she'd ever find anything funny again.

"There's nothing he can do," she lied, "he's a corporate lawyer." Wild horses wouldn't drag the truth about her parents out of her. She wouldn't admit to anyone, even to her best friend, how her own father had refused to lift one finger to help.

Despite her tears and pleadings, he'd looked her straight in the eye and told her that this time, she'd have to take full responsibility for her own actions. At seventeen, he'd lectured, she wasn't a child anymore and if she was going to be foolish enough to be influenced by the actions and opinions of a few of her so-called friends, she could pay the piper. Her mother had been of the same opinion. "Besides, like I said, the judge wants to make an example of me."

Jennifer mumbled something sympathetic again,

but Leeanne barely heard her. In her mind, she kept seeing the judge's face, reliving the awful humiliation of standing in front of the bench and knowing she'd disgraced herself and her family. It was worse than the agony of actually being arrested and taken down to the police station in the back of a squad car. She didn't think she'd ever forget how horrible the whole thing was and how rotten and guilty it made her feel. Tears flooded her eyes again, but she blinked furiously to hold them back. Darn it, she wasn't going to cry again. At least not until she got off the phone.

"Huh?" she muttered, aware that Jennifer had just asked her a question.

"I said, where is this Lavender House place?"

"Oh, it's across town. On Twin Oaks Boulevard."

"Jeez, you really did get it in the neck, didn't you? Well, keep your doors locked," Jennifer advised. "Oh, sorry, I forgot. You won't be driving your car. But however you get there, be careful. That part of town is the pits. What time do you have to go?"

"Four o'clock," Leeanne said. Her heart sank. She'd been hoping Jennifer would offer to give her a ride. Darn. "Just a minute." She held the phone away from her ear. From outside her closed door, she could hear her mother calling from downstairs. "Jen, look, Mom's yelling at me. I've got to go. I'll call you back tonight after dinner, okay?"

"Don't bother. I won't be home, remember? The decorations committee is meeting at Terry's place tonight." Jennifer gave an embarrassed laugh. "I guess you can't make it, right?"

"Right," Leeanne said glumly. "On top of everything else, I'm grounded. At least for a while."

"Okay, then, uh, I'll see you at school tomorrow. Will you be picking me up? Oops! Sorry, forgot again. I guess you'll be riding in with your mom or something. Anyway, I'll catch a ride with Terry. See you tomorrow."

Leeanne winced. God, this was so humiliating. She wasn't sure why it had suddenly become so hard to talk to Jennifer, but it was. Maybe it was because even though Jennifer clucked her tongue sympathetically, Leeanne sometimes had the impression her best friend was secretly glad to see her in so much hot water. But that was a lousy thing to think.

As soon as she hung up, she went to the door. "I'll be there in a sec, Mom." Leeanne didn't want to leave the sanctuary of her room. Leaning against the wall, she stared at the frilly white satin and lace coverlet on her bed, the pale yellow and white flowered wallpaper with the shiny white-painted trim. A room fit for a princess, her father had once said. She didn't feel much like royalty now, though. She felt like pond scum. Facing her mom was the last thing she wanted to do now. She'd had enough sour looks and lectures to last the rest of her life. Her gaze focused on her desk and her personal computer, a gift from her parents for her fifteenth birthday. The white bookshelves, filled with volumes of her old favorite science fiction books and romances, were now hardly looked at because these days she was always too busy to read. Leeanne smiled glumly. She'd have a little more time for reading now.

"Leeanne," her mother called impatiently.

Sighing, she turned and pulled open the door. She couldn't hide up here forever. Hurrying down the stairs, she saw her mother standing by the front door, her high-heeled shoe tapping against the polished oak floor.

Eileen McNab was a tall, attractive blonde dressed in a charcoal-gray suit, blue blouse, and discreet gold earrings. She looked every inch what she was, a high-powered business executive.

"I've got a meeting tonight in Los Angeles," she said. "There's a tuna salad in the fridge for your dinner."

"You're driving to L.A. tonight?" Leeanne asked. "But isn't it kinda late?"

"I don't have much choice," her mother said bluntly. "Having to waste today in court with you put me way behind schedule."

"Uh, what about Dad?" Leeanne asked hopefully. Her relations with her parents might be strained just now, but she didn't want to spend the whole evening in an empty house.

Her mother shrugged and picked up her briefcase. "He's working late. He'll probably pick up a sandwich or something at the office."

Leeanne swallowed her disappointment. "How late do you think you'll be tonight?" she asked.

"I should be back around nine," Eileen answered, checking her pockets for her car keys. "Why?"

"Well, I just need to talk to you about something, that's all."

Eileen cocked her chin at an angle and studied her appraisingly. "If it's about your driver's license, forget it," she began.

"That's not what I wanted to talk about," Leeanne exclaimed. "But since you've brought the subject up, how am I supposed to get to this place tomorrow? Without a car, I'm kind of stuck."

"You should have thought about that before you went shoplifting," Eileen replied coolly.

"I wasn't shoplifting. I intended to pay for those earrings," she said for the thousandth time. She felt like screaming in frustration. Why wouldn't her mother believe her? Why wouldn't she give her the benefit of the doubt?

"But you didn't, did you? You were too concerned with what all your little friends would think."

"Okay, so I made a bad mistake," Leeanne said. "I'll admit it. I was wrong. But in case you haven't noticed, I'm sorta in a spot here. How am I supposed to get to this nursing home without a car?"

"Don't be ridiculous"—her mother reached for the door handle—"you can take the bus."

"The bus!"

"Yes, you know, one of those long blue and white vehicles that people without cars frequently use for transportation."

Leeanne was stunned. She'd never been on a bus

in her life. "But the nursing home is in the worst part of town."

Eileen pulled the door open. "Don't be melodramatic. Landsdale doesn't have a bad part of town," she said impatiently, brushing her daughter's protests aside. "Admittedly, the place does sound as if it's located in the heart of the poorer section, but it's hardly a gang-infested slum. Lots of people take the bus," she said breezily as she started down the walkway toward her BMW. "You'll enjoy it."

As soon as the door was closed, Leeanne slumped against it. This time, when the tears came, she didn't even try to stop them. No cheerleading, no football games, no dates with Todd Barrett, no senior year parties. No car. Oh, God, how on earth was she ever going to get through this? One stupid little mistake and her life was over.

School was awful. Leeanne clutched the bus schedule in her hand and hoisted her backpack onto the bus bench. At least, she thought, glancing down the street and not seeing anyone she knew, I've managed to avoid the humiliation of half the senior class seeing me take a bus.

No one had been nasty to her face today, but she'd seen the sympathetic glances and the knowing smirks thrown her way. Leeanne flopped down on the bench and flipped open the bright blue schedule. Her mother had handed it to her this morning at breakfast with the comment that public transportation never hurt anybody and that she'd see Leeanne tonight at home. Leeanne had been tempted to throw the darned thing in the trash, but she was walking a fine edge these days with her folks and it would be downright dumb to deliberately irritate them. Maybe if she was really good, if she really kissed up to them and didn't give them any grief, they'd at least let her have her driver's license back.

Leeanne looked at her watch and frowned. It was three-forty. She hoped that whoever ran this Lavender House wouldn't give her any static about being a little late. The next bus for Twin Oaks Boulevard wasn't due for another five minutes. That would get her to Lavender House about four-ten. It should be okay. Surely, they wouldn't expect her to take the early bus? That would mean she'd have to spend half an hour more than she had to in that neighborhood and despite her mother's assurances, that area just wasn't safe.

A few moments later the bus arrived and Leeanne climbed on board. She handed the bus driver a dollar. He looked at her like she'd grown another head. "Exact change, please," he said.

"Exact change?" She was aware of everyone staring at her.

"Yeah." He jabbed a finger at a square glass and metal contraption next to where he sat. "Whatsa matter, you never took a bus before, kid? Put sixty cents in that little box there and then you can ride my bus."

Several passengers laughed. Cheeks flaming, Leeanne dug out her wallet and took out two quarters and a dime. Dropping them in, she hurried down the aisle, almost tripping over her own feet in her haste.

There was only one empty seat and she grabbed it. Putting her backpack next to her, she stared stonily out the window. The bus pulled away. She kept on looking out the window, her heart sinking as they rode past the chic, newly built shopping area on her side of Landsdale.

Soon, the bus left the clean, swept streets and beautiful homes of the nice side of town. The farther north she rode, the smaller the houses and the tackier the strip malls and businesses became. By the time the bus made a left onto Twin Oaks Boulevard, Leeanne was wondering if she shouldn't have brought along a can of Mace.

Originally, Twin Oaks had been the town's major thoroughfare, but with the coming of the suburbs and the building crazes of the 1960s, the old business and industrial area had deteriorated into a slum. Clean, light industry and the few high-tech manufacturing companies that had come here in the late sixties had all built on the east side of Landsdale. Hordes of people fleeing the smog, crime, and traffic of southern California had soon followed and brand-new picture-perfect housing tracts had sprung up everywhere. Leeanne lived in one of the newest herself. This part of town was almost as alien to her as the surface of the moon.

As the bus headed north, she saw the rows of old Victorian homes, most of which were now converted into run-down apartment houses. They passed liquor stores and pawnshops, a storefront church and a medical building with barred windows.

Finally, after what seemed an eternity, the bus chugged to a halt for a red light at Acton Street. Her stop was here. When the light changed to green she took a breath, grabbed her backpack off the seat, and told herself it wouldn't be so bad. The bus stop was right in front of the nursing home. Maybe if she ran for it, she wouldn't get mugged. She started for the back door and came face-to-face with a tall, dark-haired boy. He was a hunk. The boy stepped back and let Leeanne in front of him. The bus sailed right on past her stop. "Hey," she called, panicked. "I want to get off here."

"Then why didn't you press the buzzer?" the driver yelled back.

Buzzer? What buzzer? Leeanne frantically looked around for a button to push but didn't see one. "It's right there," a disgusted voice said from behind her. Twirling around, she frowned at the hunk who'd distracted her in the first place.

"What's the matter," he said, reaching past her and jabbing a slim strip of plastic by the window, "haven't you ever been on a bus before?"

The bus lurched to a halt before she could come up with a snappy reply. The good-looking guy, Leeanne figured him for at least eighteen, gave her a disgusted frown, stepped past her, and got off.

She scrambled off behind him. "Damn," she muttered. She peered down the street and realized the bus had taken her at least two blocks past where she wanted to be.

Leeanne's insides clenched. She was already late. Now that stupid bus was going to make her even later. Slinging her backpack over her shoulder, she headed off. Across the street, a group of boys were playing basketball in front of an abandoned gas station. A moth-eaten hoop dangled from the top of the pole over the pumps. Wary, Leeanne picked up her pace.

She was breathing hard by the time she reached the nursing home. She paused on the sidewalk and stared up at the place where she was going to be spending most of her free time for the next six months.

Like many of the buildings on Twin Oaks, it was a huge Victorian house. But it was set back on a lush green lawn, painted a delicate lavender, and decorated with white trim. A small sign over the door said simply LAVENDER HOUSE.

Leeanne walked up the concrete walkway, up the stairs, and across the wide porch. Another sign, this one much smaller, said PLEASE RING. She rang the bell and waited.

And waited.

Leeanne jabbed the bell again. Really, what was wrong with these people? Were they all deaf? Suddenly the door flew open. An unsmiling, middle-aged woman with short frizzy blond hair, wearing a hot-pink jumpsuit, stood there. "Can I help you?" she asked coldly.

"I'm, uh, Leeanne McNab. I've been assigned

here . . ." Her voice trailed off as the woman's eyes narrowed.

"For community service," the woman finished. "You're late. I expected you ten minutes ago. Come on in."

Leeanne followed her inside. The floors were polished oak. Directly ahead of her was a high mahogany counter that served as a reception desk. To her left, she could see a living room with wood paneling and pink and white flowered wallpaper. To her right was a staircase and directly behind that a cagelike contraption that she assumed was an elevator. On the other side of the staircase was a hallway and a set of closed double oak doors. There was nothing about the place that looked at all like she'd imagined a nursing home would look.

"I'm Esther Drake, the director of Lavender House," the woman said, leading Leeanne past the double doors and down the hall. "Call me Mrs. Drake. We'll talk in my office."

They entered a small, cozy room. Inside was a desk, two chairs, a filing cabinet, and a green leather couch. The walls were papered a cheerful green and white jungle pattern; there were matching curtains at the windows and a vase of fresh daisies on the desk.

Mrs. Drake went behind the desk, sat down, and motioned Leeanne into a chair. She pulled out a notepad, flipped it open, and plucked a pen out of the holder next to the daisies. "Okay, the PO called me this morning and gave me your particulars. You've got to do three hundred hours, right?"

"Right."

"And I assume you want to get them over with as quickly as possible?"

"Yes."

"Good." She smiled. "We could use the extra help around here. We're always shorthanded. What did you get busted for?"

"Shoplifting," Leeanne mumbled. It was a word she didn't like to use. Every time she heard herself say it, her skin crawled in humiliation. "But the whole thing was just a joke," she explained hastily. "It was only a pair of earrings, uh, that's what I took. But I was going to pay for them."

Mrs. Drake snorted. "Well, whatever. But I have to tell you, we're responsible for our patients' belongings and I don't want to hear that anything's been misplaced, got it?"

Leeanne's eyes widened. She couldn't believe it! She was being treated like a common criminal. Given a warning. This was too much. "Mrs. Drake," she said politely, trying to keep her temper in check. "I'm not sure what you mean."

Mrs. Drake smiled cynically. "I think you know exactly what I mean. But just so you'll understand, I'll spell it out. I don't want to hear that anyone's wallet, purse, money, or personal stuff isn't exactly where it's supposed to be. Got it?"

Humiliated, Leeanne felt her cheeks flame. Did that mean if someone else stole something or if a patient mislaid a paperback that she'd get blamed for it? "But that's not fair," she said. "I'm not a thief."

"Sure you are," Mrs. Drake said casually, "and not a very good one either. You got caught, didn't you? Besides, life's not fair. Working here will get that through your head. But don't worry, we're not going to string you up or tar and feather you if someone's Nestle Crunch bar goes missing. Just do your work and keep your nose clean, okay?"

Leeanne clamped down on the sick, hot anger surging in her stomach. She really didn't have much choice in the matter. "Okay. Uh, exactly what will I be doing?"

"Let's work out your schedule first," Mrs. Drake said. She pulled a three-ring binder out of her bottom drawer and plonked it on the desk. Flipping it open, she scanned the page. "Let's see, Sundays are already taken care of, we've got Mrs. Deering." She peered up at Leeanne. "What time do you get out of school?"

"Two-thirty."

She frowned. "Then why were you late today?"

Leeanne shifted nervously. She didn't want to admit she'd spent over an hour trying to con one of her friends into giving her a ride. "Uh, I had to go to the library and get some books."

"But you can be here by three-thirty from now on, right?"

She did some quick calculations in her head, trying to remember exactly when the early bus came. It should be okay. "Right."

"Good. Then Monday through Thursday you can do a three-thirty to six, Fridays till five-thirty, and a full eight hours on Saturdays." Mrs. Drake was already scribbling away in the three-ring binder. "That's twenty hours a week . . . that should leave you evenings and Sundays for your studies."

Leeanne's heart sank all the way to her toes. God, this was worse than she'd imagined. She wouldn't have time to do anything after school and by the time she got home at night, there'd be just enough time left to gulp a quick dinner and do her homework. She wasn't sure what she'd expected, but hearing it all spelled out like this made her sick to her stomach. "Okay," she mumbled.

"And don't be late again," Mrs. Drake said. She stood up. "Our patients need to know they can rely on people to be here when they're supposed to be." She studied Leeanne intently for a moment. "You don't have a drug problem, do you?"

"Of course not."

"Good, because the drugs are kept under lock and key."

Leeanne was offended. She'd never even been tempted to do drugs. But she was pretty sure Mrs. Drake wouldn't much believe that either.

"Come on." Mrs. Drake came out from behind the desk. "We're already behind schedule. I'll give you a tour of the place and get you started."

Obediently Leeanne stood up. "Where can I put my backpack?" she asked as she followed the director down the hall.

"Dump it in the closet." Mrs. Drake stopped and opened a door.

Relieved of her pack, Leeanne tried to keep everything straight. Mrs. Drake took her to the kitchen first. A tall, ebony-skinned woman wearing a print housedress and a white cook's apron was peeling vegetables at the sink. "Mrs. Thomas," Mrs. Drake said, "I'd like you to meet Leeanne McNab, she'll be working here for the next few months."

"I'm pleased to meet you," Mrs. Thomas said, wiping her hand on her apron and extending it to Leeanne.

Leeanne clumsily shook Mrs. Thomas's hand. It was the first time in her life she could ever remember shaking hands with anyone and she wasn't very good at it. "Pleased to meet you too," she mumbled, suddenly embarrassed because she was sure from the knowing look in the woman's eyes that she knew exactly *why* Leeanne was here.

"Dinner is served at six-thirty," Mrs. Drake said. "One of your duties before you leave for the day is helping Mrs. Thomas get the trays ready for those patients who want to eat in their rooms."

"Does that mean some of the patients eat in the dining room?"

"Yes, if they're feeling up to it."

"What other duties will I have?" Leeanne gritted her teeth. She was pretty sure that as the new kid on the block she'd get most of the dirty work.

"It'll vary," Mrs. Drake replied, heading for a door that led off the kitchen to a huge utility. "Today I want you to fold towels and sheets. Our laundry boy didn't show up today."

Folding linens didn't sound too bad, she thought. It beat the hell out of emptying bedpans.

After the kitchen, the tour continued through the dining room, the laundry, the medical supply room, the nurse's station, and the three sitting rooms. Leeanne got more and more confused. Where were the old ladies and their wheelchairs? Where were the IV bottles and the heart monitors and the rehabilitation stuff?

"Uh, where are all the patients?" Leeanne asked as they started up the stairs.

"Some of them are resting in their rooms," Mrs. Drake said, "and some of them are out."

"Out?"

"Yes." Mrs. Drake stopped on the top of the landing. "This isn't a prison, you know. If they're able, some of the patients go out shopping or over to the library or to the coffee shop across the street."

"Sorry," Leeanne muttered. "But I didn't realize nursing homes were so . . . so . . . flexible."

"Nursing home?" Mrs. Drake looked puzzled. "This isn't a nursing home."

"Then what is it?" Leeanne was tired of feeling like an idiot.

"It's a hospice. People come here to die."

Chapter
Two

September 19

Dear Diary,

As my mom always says when she's trying really hard to be cool, what a bummer! Sometimes Mom likes to pretend she's still a hippie from the sixties. Though I must admit, imagining her in a headband and bell-bottoms is mind-boggling. But, as I was saying, what a bummer. I'm working at a hospice. It's bad enough that I have to do three hundred hours, but having to do them in a place where people go to die is too much. Talk about depressing. It wouldn't be so bad if it was just a bunch of old people—I mean that's awful enough, but at least with them, you'd kinda feel like they'd had a crack at life. But this place has people of all ages, even someone who's close to my age. Luckily, I didn't have to meet this kid. Mrs. Drake kept me so busy fixing dinner trays and folding sheets that I didn't get much of a chance to meet anyone. The place is the pits. Oh, it doesn't look bad or anything like that, but there's no way I'm going to do my community service there. It's too morbid. I don't care if it's the last thing I do, I'm going to figure a way to get out of Lavender House. The director hates me, it's in a lousy part of town, and I don't think I want to spend the next four months hanging around people who are waiting to die. I'll have to think of something.

About the only good thing that happened yesterday was that I did see a real hunk on the bus. But he was kind of rude.

Leeanne heard her mother yelling from downstairs that it was time to go. She shoved her diary in the drawer of her bedside table, grabbed her backpack, and ran for the stairs.

She and her mother didn't talk much on the drive to school. Leeanne found that depressing too. She could remember when they talked all the time. But ever since her mom had started working, they'd had less and less to say to each other. Sometimes, Leeanne thought, as she glanced at her mom out of the corner of her eye, she felt like the two of them were on different planets.

Leeanne spotted Jennifer as soon as she got out of the car. She was standing beneath a huge oak tree in front of the school. With her wide hazel eyes, slim figure, and picture-perfect brown hair,

Jennifer was one of the most popular girls at Landsdale High.

"Hi," she said as Leeanne drew close. "How did it go yesterday?"

"The pits," Leeanne replied. She took a quick look around to see if anyone was staring at her. Most of the kids stood around in front of the two-story building in small groups. She didn't see any overt glances thrown her way. No one was paying any attention to her at all. Maybe by now, she was old news. "The place is really creepy and it's in an incredibly lousy part of town. I'll be lucky if I don't get mugged."

"What are the people like?" Jennifer asked.

"I didn't meet anyone except the director and a couple of the staff people." Leeanne saw Todd heading toward her. She smiled. "And they weren't anything to write home about."

"Hi, Leeanne, Jen." Todd grinned at both of them. "How's it going? I heard you got stuck doing time at a nursing home."

Leeanne threw Jennifer a quick, irritated frown, but Jennifer was too busy gaping at Todd to notice. He was worth looking at, Leeanne thought. Tall, blond, incredibly handsome, and one of the best football players Landsdale had ever had, he was definitely the coolest guy at school. He and Leeanne had dated a few times but he'd made it clear their relationship wasn't exclusive. He dated lots of girls. But Leeanne liked him anyway. One of her fantasies was that he'd discover he was desperately in love with her.

"Okay," Leeanne replied, embarrassed. It was one thing to tell yourself that you weren't really a thief, but having to actually face people after you'd been caught was damned hard. "Uh, I'm hoping it will all turn out to be a good experience for me." She might as well see if she could pick up some points by playing it cool. Everyone loved a saint. "I mean, I made a mistake, sure. But things have a way of working out for the best."

"That's not what you were saying just now," Jennifer put in quickly. "You said the place was lousy."

"I said it was in a lousy part of town," Leeanne said. What was wrong with Jennifer? Was her best friend trying to make her look like an idiot? It was bad enough that Jen had obviously kept the phone lines buzzing last night, Leeanne expected that. Keeping secrets wasn't Jen's strong point. But she didn't expect Jen to deliberately try to make her look stupid in front of Todd.

"Where's this place at?" Todd asked.

"In the old part of town, on Twin Oaks Boulevard."

"Wow, that is a crummy neighborhood." Todd gazed at her sympathetically. "You'd better be careful, Leeanne. A girl who looks like you could be an easy target. You're awfully good-looking. Watch your back and stay out of dark alleys."

Leeanne smiled gratefully. She knew she was pretty. Slender, green-eyed blondes didn't grow on trees. But it was nice having someone say it. "I should be okay," she said. "I'm careful."

"Are you coming to the game Friday night?"

Leeanne couldn't tell if Todd was talking to her or to Jennifer. Jennifer had no such problem. "I am," she said boldly. "But Leeanne won't be able to."

"Maybe I can," Leeanne interjected. She didn't know what Jen was up to but she was getting tired of it. "I get off at five-thirty on Fridays."

"Aren't you grounded?" Jennifer picked up her backpack and slung it over her shoulder. She smiled innocently at Leeanne. "And how would you get there without a car or a driver's license?"

"Uh, maybe I could give you a lift?" Todd put in. "It's a home game so I don't have to be at the field until six."

"That's okay," Leeanne said, her heart sinking faster than her grade in physics. But she was deeply hurt by Jennifer's attitude. Maybe they weren't such good friends as she'd always thought. "I am grounded," she admitted. "At least for the rest of the month. But I appreciate the offer."

"You can give me a lift," Jennifer said.

Todd ignored her. "Working in a nursing home shouldn't be too bad. My grandma's in one and it's a pretty nice place."

Leeanne decided she might as well tell the truth. There was no point in lying. Besides, even though Lavender House was awful, she had started to feel a little guilty about her attitude. Knowing you were going to die must be the absolute worst. "It's not really a nursing home," she explained. "It's a hospice."

"What's that?" Jennifer asked.

"A place where people go to die," Todd replied, his attention still on Leeanne. "Man, that's really weird."

"Weird?" Leeanne asked. "Why?"

He shrugged and she couldn't help but notice how broad his shoulders were beneath his letterman's jacket. "Because of your age."

"My age? What's that got to do with it?"

"Everything," Todd said. "You're a first offender and you committed a nonviolent crime." He broke off and looked a little embarrassed. "I hope you don't mind, but well, I happened to mention you to my uncle."

She did mind but there wasn't much she could do about it. Leeanne was fairly certain she'd been the topic of a lot of conversations among her friends and their families. "That's okay."

He gave her a grateful smile. "Anyway, according to my uncle, and he ought to know because he works for the Probation Department, you should have been put somewhere like a hospital or a community center. As a matter of fact, he was pretty sure that's where you were going to be assigned. Are you sure they didn't make some kind of mistake? It wouldn't be the first time they've screwed up, you know."

"Oh, for God's sake," Jennifer interrupted. "What's the big deal? The only thing she'll be doing is emptying bedpans or changing a few sheets."

Todd shook his head. "Putting Leeanne in a place where she's going to watch people wait to die is about the dumbest thing they could do. That kind of thing can really mess up your head."

"That's silly," Jennifer said.

"No it's not," Todd insisted. "You need special training to handle working in a hospice. I know, my other uncle's a minister. He's always talking about how easy it is to burn out when you work with terminally ill people." He looked at Leeanne. "The probation people must have made a mistake. There's no way they should have sent you to a hospice. No way at all. Do you want me to ask my uncle about it?"

An idea sprouted in the back of Leeanne's mind. There might be a way out of all this after all. Todd was right. Working at Lavender House could be terribly damaging. Burnout, depression, sleeplessness, loss of appetite. The possibilities were endless.

"That's really nice of you, Todd," she replied, giving him her warmest smile. "Maybe you should ask him. I mean, if the Probation Department made a mistake, I'd sure like to know about it."

The bell rang and all three of them headed into the building. Leeanne smiled to herself as she half listened to Jennifer's chatter. Wasn't it lucky that she and Todd had had this little talk? Suddenly she saw a ray of hope. She'd get away from that place if it was the last thing she ever did.

Leeanne made sure she caught the early bus that afternoon. It let her off at the bus stop at five to three. She glanced up the street, trying to decide whether to show up a half an hour early or to go have a Coke at the coffee shop on the end of the block. A group of boys walked by and stopped just a few feet away from the front of the hospice. They didn't look friendly. That made up her mind for her, she scurried toward the corner. Maybe they'd be gone by the time her shift was due to start.

Frowning, Leeanne pushed through the heavy glass doors and headed straight toward the counter. The place was clean, but that was about all you could say for it. Gray, heavy-tracked lino on the floors, swivel stools with cracked red leather seats, and a green and gray chrome-plated counter that looked like it had been new during World War II. She sat down on one of the stools, dug her physics text out of her pack, and flipped it open. She might as well get some of her homework done.

"What'll it be?"

Leeanne looked up straight into the eyes of the rude hunk who'd been on the bus yesterday. A white apron was wrapped around his waist and he was holding a pad and pencil. Up close he was even cuter than she'd thought. Gray eyes, dark hair, and a set of shoulders broad enough to make a girl's heart skip. "Uh, just a Coke, please."

"Anything else?"

She shook her head and breathed a sigh of relief. He hadn't recognized her as the idiot who didn't even know how to open a bus door, she thought, watching him from the corner of her eyes.

"You a student?" he asked as he set the Coke in front of her.

"I'm a senior at Landsdale." Her heartbeat picked up. His voice was cool. Real cool.

"Hey, Nathan," a man called from the other end of the counter. He held up his cup. "Can we have some more coffee?"

Nathan didn't speak to her again, but Leeanne was conscious of him glancing at her whenever he thought she wasn't looking. She pretended to find her physics textbook madly fascinating.

Fifteen minutes later, she paid her check and left. The group of boys was gone when she got to Lavender House but she hurried inside anyway. In this neighborhood, it paid to be off the street.

Mrs. Drake hustled her upstairs the minute she walked in the door. "Today I want you to meet the patients," she said.

Leeanne slowed her steps.

"Sometimes we do things for them, you know," Mrs. Drake continued. If she was aware of Leeanne's dawdling, she didn't let it show. At the landing she stopped and waited.

"What kind of things?" Leeanne asked, her voice apprehensive. Oh, God, she thought, I'm not a nurse. Surely they won't expect me to give shots or put in catheters. But she wouldn't put it past them, so far she hadn't seen anyone remotely resembling a doctor or nurse.

Mrs. Drake smiled slightly. "Don't look so worried. We're not going to have you do brain surgery. Some of our patients like to be read to and some of our people like to go out for walks, but they need a little help. And some people just like company. That is part of what a volunteer does. A little of everything. After you meet everyone, you can fix up the dinner trays."

"Oh," Leeanne said, shrugging. "I guess I can manage that."

"Good," Mrs. Drake said briskly. "And before I forget, make sure you remind me to introduce you to Mrs. Meeker. She's the day duty nurse around here. She dispenses the painkillers and medicine and makes our patients as comfortable as possible."

Leeanne nodded and then glanced behind her at the sound of heels clicking against the stairs. A heavily made-up middle-aged woman, her black hair teased into a mountain, came up the stairs toward them. She wore a tight green spandex pantsuit cinched with a cherry-red belt, dangling rhinestone earrings, and three-inch sling-backed clear plastic heels.

"Polly," Mrs. Drake said, "this is Leeanne McNab, the girl I told you about. Leeanne, this is Polly Dickson, one of our best volunteers."

"Nice to meet you Leeanne," the woman said, extending her hand.

"Thank you," Leeanne replied, trying not to stare at the gold glitter decorating Polly's long red fingernails, "I'm pleased to meet you too."

"I've got to get to a meeting," Mrs. Drake said. "Polly'll show you the ropes." She hurried down the steps.

"Have you met any of the patients yet?" Polly asked.

"No, I've just learned where everything is and done dinner trays."

"Okeydoke." Polly grinned and took Leeanne's arm. "Come on, we'll start with Mr. Kenworthy first. He's nice." She started down the hall.

Leeanne was suddenly scared. What did you say to someone who was dying? How did you act? Did you pretend that everything was just fine? "What's he, uh . . . got?"

"ALS. Lou Gehrig's disease. He moved in here when his wife passed away and there wasn't anyone else to take care of him." She stopped in front of the last door down a long hallway, knocked softly, and then pushed inside.

Leeanne followed. The room was bright and sunny with green and yellow flowered wallpaper, sheer curtains at the open window, and a large-screen TV. A man with thin black hair and glasses was sitting in a wheelchair beside a regulation hospital bed.

"Hi, Jake," Polly called cheerfully. "How's it going today?"

"Fine." His words were so slurred the word came out as "Fnnn." His gaze, but not his body, shifted so that he could stare at Leeanne.

"This is Leeanne McNab," Polly said. "She's a volunteer."

"Hi," Leeanne felt a rush of pity and struggled not to let it show on her face. Luckily, she and Polly didn't linger after the introduction. Worse, she couldn't think of a thing to say.

Polly introduced her to three more patients, two

with cancer and one with AIDS. Leeanne tried not to think about why they were here and why they weren't being taken care of by their families. She didn't want to have to think about the answers. It was too depressing. But surprisingly enough, the people she met were all smiling and cheerful. Jamie Brubaker, the cancer patient, was on his way out to the movies.

"I'll introduce you to Gabriel next," Polly said, leading her toward a room set back by itself off a small staircase at the end of the hall. "He could probably use some company about now."

The room was much like the others, except that it had more windows. A dark-haired boy was lying on the bed reading a magazine. He looked up as they came in. "Hi, Polly, how's it going?"

Polly giggled. "Same as always. I've brought you one of our newest volunteers. Leeanne McNab meet Gabriel Mendoza."

"Hi," he said coolly.

"Hi," she replied. He was very thin, she noticed, and dressed in a heavy pair of corduroy jeans and a thick wool shirt. His hair was jet-black, his skin a warm honey color, and his eyes a rich, velvety chocolate-brown. But it wasn't the unusual darkness of his eyes that startled her, it was the way he looked at her. For a brief moment she had the funny feeling that he could see all the way into her soul. Leeanne had to drag her gaze away from his.

"I'll leave you two to get acquainted," Polly said. "Maybe you can play cards or something. Gabriel, you be nice now. We don't want you running off the help."

"I only run off the flakes," he replied, never taking his gaze off Leeanne.

Leeanne panicked. She didn't want to be left alone with him. And she didn't know why. But Polly had already gone.

He continued to stare at her. "So, where do you go to school?" he finally asked.

"Landsdale High. Where do you go?" She felt like biting her tongue—obviously, as frail as he was, he didn't go anywhere. "Uh, I'm sorry, that was a dumb question."

"I used to go to Tufts," he replied. "But that seems like a long time ago. I graduated last year. How come you're volunteering in a place like this?"

She shifted uneasily. For some reason, she was ashamed to admit she wasn't exactly "volunteering." "Well, I wanted to do something to help." She gazed around the room, not wanting to meet his eyes. There were bookcases under the windows and her attention was caught by the silver-gray cover of one of her favorite books. "Is that Harry Harrison's book?" she asked, pointing toward the top of the bookcase.

"Yeah, it's one of the 'Eden' series. You read science fiction?"

Leeanne hurried toward the bookcase. The movement gave her something to do, made it possible for her not to have to look at him. "I used to read more than I do now," she said, picking up the book. The cover was creased and the pages dog-eared in spots; it looked well read and well loved. She suddenly remembered how much pleasure reading used to give her. "But I'm so busy now, it's hard to find the time."

"Oh, yeah, with all your volunteering," he stressed the last word sarcastically, "it must be tough."

Leeanne glanced up sharply. "What does that mean?"

He grinned and his thin face was transformed. His eyes gleamed impishly. "It means, cut the con job. Everyone knows you're not here out of the kindness of your heart. You got busted and this is your community service."

"That doesn't mean I won't do a good job," she said defensively.

He shrugged, as though he didn't care much one way or the other. "What'd you get busted for?"

"Shoplifting." She put the book down. "But I wasn't actually intending to steal. It was only a prank."

"Yeah, couple of my friends pulled a prank like that," he sneered, "only the cops called it Grand Theft Auto. They didn't get community service. They're both pulling time at CYA."

"A pair of earrings isn't like stealing a car," she protested.

"They weren't stealing that car, they were only joyriding," he snorted. "But they were poor and Hispanic, not rich and white."

"That's a lousy thing to say," she snapped. Then

she clamped her mouth shut. Damn. This kid was dying. She didn't even know what was wrong with him. Maybe she should keep her mouth shut no matter how obnoxious he was. She didn't want him getting upset or keeling over on her.

"The truth is often lousy," he said. "Especially for my buddies. They got two years. You got three hundred hours."

A mixture of emotions rolled in her stomach. Anger at his attitude, shame, and humiliation. What did he expect her to do, apologize for not going to jail. "I'd better go help with the dinner trays," she said.

She ran into Polly on the first-floor landing. "Finished already?" Polly asked as she pulled a stack of towels off a cart.

"I think he was getting tired," Leeanne lied. "What's wrong with him?"

"Bum ticker," Polly replied.

"A bad heart?" Leeanne frowned. "Couldn't he get a transplant?"

Polly shook her head. "Gabriel had some kind of bad virus infection. It messed up the valves or something like that. Whatever it was, he doesn't qualify for a transplant. Not that he'd have much luck getting one anyway. Not in the time he has left."

"How old is he?"

"Eighteen." Polly smiled sadly.

Leeanne didn't ask any more questions. She didn't really want to know the answers. Gabriel hadn't been the nicest person she'd ever met, but she didn't like to think of what he was facing. Jeez, he was an obnoxious creep. But he was only eighteen.

She spent a half hour helping Polly put fresh towels out and met most of the other residents at the same time. There were twelve people at Lavender House and all of them had the same thing in common: they were dying.

Polly took her downstairs, stuck her head into Mrs. Drake's office, and told her she'd introduce Leeanne to the nurse. Lavender House had an RN on the premises twenty-four hours a day. Someone had to be around to dispense medication, not medicine that made people well, but drugs that helped them cope with the pain.

After that, Leeanne fixed dinner trays with Mrs. Thomas and in the process found out that the cook had two grown kids. Her daughter was going to law school and her son was studying to be an electrical engineer.

Time passed so quickly that Polly had to stick her head into the kitchen and remind Leeanne that it was time to go. Grabbing her things, she hurried out to the bus stop.

All the way home, Leeanne thought about how she should play everything. Talking to Todd had started her thinking. There was a way out of this, there was a way to avoid having to go back to that place. She leaned her head against the bus window. Outside, the sky was rapidly darkening. Streetlights were already on and the traffic was heavy.

She got off at her bus stop and hurried home.

* * *

Leeanne pushed shrimp and rice around her plate. It wasn't that she didn't like the food, she did, but she wanted to make sure her parents noticed how bad her appetite had become.

"You'd better hurry, Leeanne," her mother said, reaching for another hot roll, "you've got homework to do."

"I'm finished." She pushed her chair back and got up.

"You haven't eaten much," her father said, glancing up from his own plate to frown at hers. "Look at all that food you're wasting. Did you eat something that spoiled your dinner?"

"No, I haven't had a thing since lunch except a Coke. I'm just not very hungry," she replied, cautioning herself to play it cool.

"Don't worry about her, Gerald," her mother said, shooting her husband an exasperated look, "she's perfectly healthy."

"Okay, if you say so. But I still think she ought to eat more." Gerald McNab glanced at his daughter. He was a plump, middle-aged man with dark hair sprinkled with gray, brown eyes, and heavy eyebrows. "How was the nursing home?" he asked politely.

Leeanne shrugged. She had to be very, very careful here. Her parents were still pretty angry at her. If she wanted to gain their sympathy and get dear old daddy to pull a few strings, she had to play this just right. "It's fine." She gave him a wan smile. "Kind of sad too."

"Nursing homes usually are," he said bluntly. He shoveled another forkful of shrimp into his mouth.

Leeanne hesitated. She sensed that this wasn't the time to let them know that Lavender House wasn't a nursing home. In their current frame of mind, they'd probably think that doing time at a hospice was her just deserts. No, she'd save that until they were a little less pissed off.

Leeanne toyed with her food a few more minutes and her frustration grew. Her parents were rattling on about their day, neither of them seemed to notice how sad and depressed she was. Darn. Well, she'd just have to try harder.

"Hadn't you better get started on your homework," her mother said, glancing at her watch.

Leeanne gave up. Tonight she could have the Angel of Death himself hovering over her shoulder and she didn't think her parents would be all that concerned. Man, they were still really pissed. She'd better give it a few days, a week even. "Right, I've got a physics quiz tomorrow."

The next morning she had to walk to school, which made her late. She was hurrying up the stairs when the first bell rang. Jennifer hadn't called her, she was going to be late for her first class, and she hadn't been able to get Gabriel Mendoza and the other patients at Lavender House out of her mind.

Her mood didn't improve when Mr. Campbell, her honors English teacher, announced that they would have a book report due the following Monday.

The entire class groaned, but old Campbell wasn't moved. "This is an honors class," he said, picking up a piece of chalk and moving toward the blackboard, "so none of you should have a problem getting a book finished."

"But we're halfway through this week already," Kimberly Rand spoke up. "That's only a few days."

"Give up TV," Campbell said.

"Can we read any book we want?" someone asked from the back of the class.

"As long as it's a real book with real words instead of pictures, I don't care." Campbell gave them a sly smile. "And do try to avoid getting me in trouble with the Board of Education. *Catcher in the Rye* is fine but Henry Miller or Terry Southern is completely off-limits. Try to stick to books they actually have in the school library."

Leeanne sighed. The Landsdale Unified School District wasn't known for being very liberal about what books were suitable for high school kids. The selection was going to be pretty lame. Then she remembered that she'd gotten the first of the "Eden" series from the library. What the heck, she thought, taking out her pencil. If push comes to shove I can always write a report on that.

She didn't see Jennifer all day, but Todd caught up with her just as she was coming out of the library.

"Hi," he said. "How's it going?"

"Fine."

"Look, that offer for a ride to the game Friday night is still open."

Leeanne wished with all her heart she could go, but asking her folks to let her off restriction now would really mess things up. But she liked Todd. Darn. "That's really nice of you," she replied, giving him a bright smile, "and if I wasn't grounded, I'd say 'yes' in a fast minute."

"I understand," he said. "Maybe we can get together once you're off restriction."

She opened her mouth to agree, but before she could say a word, the funniest image popped into her head. Nathan, the hunk from the bus. Leeanne blinked and then smiled uneasily as she saw Todd's expression turn puzzled. "Yeah, that'd be nice."

"Okay, make sure you let me know when you're able to go out. Oh, I'm going to be seeing my uncle on Sunday. I'll ask him about Lavender House."

"Oh." Leeanne shrugged. "Don't bother. My dad'll take care of it."

"You sure?"

She nodded. Then she wondered what on earth she was doing? Surely she could use all the help she could get in getting free of Lavender House.

"Okay. See you later." He waved and walked off toward the quad.

Leeanne stood staring at him for a moment wondering why she hadn't given him more encouragement. But all sorts of silly things were jumbling up in her mind. Nathan, Polly, the patients at the hospice, Gabriel sneering at her. For a moment she'd felt funny. She bit her lip trying to pinpoint the odd feeling. But she couldn't. Leeanne gave up and hurried off to her next class.

Chapter
Three

September 21

Dear Diary,

I didn't have time to write this morning, so I'm playing catch up as I wait for the bus. Things aren't working out as I'd planned. I've got a book report due on Monday and the library doesn't have the book I need. Todd asked me again about going out . . . maybe one of my fantasies has come true and he's crazy about me. But the weird thing is, I'm not so sure I want to go out with him. I couldn't stop thinking about Nathan last night. And it's not just because he's a hunk, either. I feel funny about everything. I kept thinking about that rude jerk, Gabriel, too. On top of that, my parents are so dense they can't see what's right under their noses. Mom didn't even notice that I didn't eat breakfast this morning. If this keeps up much longer, I'm going to starve to death before they get it through their thick heads that I'm severely depressed. Or is that clinically depressed? Whatever, the plan doesn't seem to be working. Maybe I'll have to lay it on a bit thicker.

Leeanne heard the squeal of air brakes signaling the approach of the bus. She jammed her diary in her backpack, stood up, and dug out the exact change from the pocket of her jeans. That was another irritant, now she always had to make sure she had enough quarters and dimes for the bus.

Instead of getting off at the stop in front of the hospice, Leeanne waited for the stop opposite the diner. She ran across the street and pushed in through the heavy glass door. Sliding onto a stool, she glanced around, looking for Nathan.

The place was almost empty. A couple of the booths had customers and there was a man hunched over the newspaper down the counter from her.

Nathan appeared through a set of swing doors behind the counter. He was carrying stacked trays filled with glassware. Leeanne couldn't help noticing the way the muscles of his arms bulged. She hoped she wasn't being too obvious. But, hey, she did have a half hour to kill and it wasn't like there was much to do around here.

She took out her French book, flipped it open, and tried to concentrate on conjugating verbs. But it was impossible. She was too aware of Nathan. Without being obvious, she peeked at him out of the corner of her eye as he unloaded the trays onto the back counter. When he turned around and headed toward her, she quickly lowered her gaze.

"Hi," he said, whipping out his pad and pencil. "What'll it be?"

"Just a Coke." She stared at his back as he got her drink. His movements were sure and steady as he filled her glass with ice and shoved it under the dispenser. He looked like a guy with a lot of self-confidence.

Nathan swung around and put the drink in front of her. "Thank you," she said.

He grinned. "You don't live around here." It was a statement, not a question.

"No." She peeled the paper off the straw and slipped it into her glass. "I live on the east side." Play it cool, Leeanne, she told herself. Play it real cool.

"So what are you doing over here?"

"I'm working as a volunteer down the street. But my shift doesn't start until half past."

"Volunteering? You mean at the hospice, Lavender House?" he asked.

Leeanne smiled. "Yes, does that surprise you?"

He shrugged. "You seem kinda young, that's all."

"I'm seventeen," she said, her confidence growing by the minute. He was impressed, she could see it in his eyes. She decided to lay it on a bit thicker. "Besides, I think people should help each other, don't you?"

"Sure." Nathan reached behind him for the coffeepot and poured more in the cup of the man at the end of the counter. The man grunted his thanks. "But between work and school," he continued, "helping out my fellow man is a luxury I can't afford. Not that I'm putting you down or anything. I think it's great."

"It does feel pretty good," Leeanne said.

"Yeah, I know what you mean. We do a little of it ourselves. Henry, that's the owner here, sometimes has me take over a cake or a pie to the hospice. It's not much, but it feels like we're doing our bit. Some of the patients come in for coffee too. If we're not busy, I'll shoot the breeze or play a quick game of cards with them."

"That's really nice." Leeanne took a sip of Coke. "Where do you go to school?"

"Landsdale JC. I'm hoping to go to UC Santa Barbara after that," he said. "What's your name?"

"Leeanne McNab. What's yours?" she asked even though she already knew.

"Nathan Lourie." He smiled broadly. "So I guess we'll be seeing a lot of you around here. Uh, about the other day, on the bus."

"What about it?" Darn, Leeanne thought, he did remember. Now he'd think she was an idiot.

"Uh, I'm sorry I was so rude, but I was late for work."

"Oh, that's okay."

In between customers, they talked until it was time for Leeanne to leave. She found out that Nathan lived with his widowed mother, took a full course load at junior college, and hoped to one day be a psychologist. She could tell he was interested in her, but she thought it too bad that he didn't have his own car. Oh, well, she thought as she paid her check and waved good-bye, maybe if they started dating her parents would relent and give her her license back.

Her spirits were high as she climbed the steps to Lavender House. She even had a wide smile for Mrs. Drake. But her good mood changed when she was told what her duties were. Cleaning bathrooms. She hoped she remembered how. The last time she'd cleaned a bathroom was when she was twelve. They'd had a cleaning woman since then.

It wasn't as bad as she'd thought it would be she decided ninety minutes later. She rinsed the sink in Jamie Brubaker's room and pulled off her rubber gloves. Opening the bathroom door, she saw Jamie, an AIDS patient, resting quietly. She'd spent ten minutes talking with him when she'd arrived and had been surprised at what an interesting person he was. He'd been an airline pilot before getting sick.

She was glad Jamie was asleep though, even their little chat had tired him out.

Outside, she put her pail of cleaning supplies on the cart and checked the room off. Only two more to go and then she could go down and do dinner trays. She liked doing trays, at least when she was putting out plates and silverware she had someone to talk to. Leeanne pushed the cart down the hall, frowning as she realized the next bathroom on her list was in Gabriel's room. As instructed, she knocked softly and then peeked inside. If the patients were sleeping she'd been told not to disturb them if she didn't have to.

Gabriel was sitting at the window. "Come on in," he called softly.

"I'm, uh, going to clean your bathroom," she explained.

"Be my guest." He gave her a wide grin.

Leeanne put her bucket of supplies on the tile floor and started to close the door.

"Leave it open," Gabriel called.

Her head came up and she saw him standing just outside. "Why?" she asked. "You get some kind of kick out of seeing me scrub sinks?"

"Not sinks," he said, leaning against the frame, "toilets."

"Very funny." She was tempted to slam the door in his face, but the truth was, she was glad to have someone to talk to. "How come you're not in bed?"

"I'm not tired. And I'm in the mood for company. Even yours."

"Thanks a lot." Leeanne sprinkled the cleanser in the tub. "You must really be desperate if you want to talk to me." She was suddenly annoyed. Okay, maybe she was a little better off and maybe she wasn't here out of the goodness of her heart, but that didn't give him the right to be so . . . so . . . sneering. "What's the matter, don't you have any friends?"

He laughed and pushed a lock of hair off his face. The movement drew her gaze to his hands and arms. His forearms were so thin they looked like flesh-covered sticks and the veins on his hands were clearly outlined against his dark skin. Her irritation vanished as she saw the pitiful effects of his illness. She'd bet her last allowance that underneath the black sweats he wore the rest of him was equally wasted.

"Most of my buddies live down in L.A. Unlike your friends, Daddy didn't buy them a set of wheels on their sixteenth birthday."

"I'll have you know I take the bus," Leeanne snapped as her sympathy vanished.

"Yeah, but I'll bet you've got a car."

She clamped her mouth shut and stuck her cleaning cloth under the faucet. Dying or not, he was a jerk. The fact that he was absolutely right about her was totally irrelevant. So she had a car. So what? Lots of people had cars. Why should she feel guilty because her folks worked hard and gave her nice things?

"You do, don't you," he continued. "What is it? A snazzy little convertible, something expensive that Daddy didn't want you driving into a neighborhood like this?"

"It's not a convertible," she said, turning on the water and splashing it around the sides of the tub. "It's a compact."

"How come you're taking the bus then?"

She started to tell him it was for the reason he'd already said, because she didn't want to bring it into this neighborhood, but oddly, she felt funny lying to him. "When I got arrested my parents took my driver's license."

"Tough break," he mumbled, but Leeanne didn't hear any genuine sympathy in his voice. "But at least when you've served your time, you'll get it back. How long you gonna be here anyway?"

"I got three hundred hours of community service," she said, getting up from the floor, "and I'm here twenty hours a week. You figure it out. If you need any help, I've got a calculator in my backpack."

"Keep your calculator, I made straight A's in math," he said, laughing again.

That did surprise her. "You did?"

"Yeah," he said proudly. "What did you think? That everyone with a Hispanic name does nothing but gang-bang and drive low-riders."

"I didn't think that," she said, incensed that he should accuse her of thinking in racial stereotypes.

"Then why'd you look so surprised?"

"I just was, that's all." But he was too close to the mark for comfort. Leeanne was startled at herself. She'd never thought she had an ounce of prejudice in her whole body. But if that were true, why *had* she been surprised when he'd told her about his math grade.

"Okay," he admitted cautiously. "Maybe you didn't think I was a gang-banging lowlife."

"And maybe I shouldn't have been so surprised," she said, compelled for some weird reason to be honest with this kid. "Anyway, I'm sorry if I offended you."

"No sweat." Gabriel nodded. "I shouldn't have jumped down your throat so fast either. I guess I'm a little sensitive when I'm around Anglos. But just for the record, I was a straight A student all my life. I got a full scholarship to UCSD." He shrugged and dropped his gaze to the floor tiles. "Course, now I'll never get to use it."

Leeanne stared at him. She had no idea what to say. She didn't like him much, but right now, she was overwhelmed with sadness. A full scholarship and he'd never get to set foot on a college campus. She thought of her own three point four grade point average and how her parents were always nagging her to bring it up. Jeez, it just wasn't fair. Jerk or not, Gabriel Mendoza had obviously worked his tail off to go to college. No one pulled a four point 0 unless they really busted their buns. "Man, I'm really sorry," she said. "You must have really worked hard. Four-ohs don't grow on trees."

"Don't be sorry for me," he said, lifting his gaze to meet hers. His eyes were dark pools of ancient wisdom. Infinitely sad and infinitely understanding. Leeanne felt a lump form in her throat, her lips moved as she struggled to say something . . . but there weren't any words. There was nothing to say.

"Sometimes," Gabriel continued softly, "you get the bear. Sometimes the bear gets you."

Leeanne tried to push those last few moments with Gabriel out of her mind. She pulled off her rubber gloves and stared at her hands. The flesh was red and irritated. Despite her precautions, she wasn't very good at keeping the water out. She'd have to remember to use plenty of hand lotion when she got home.

"Sometimes the bear gets you." His words echoed in her ears as she put the cleaning supplies back in the closet. She could hear Mrs. Thomas singing softly to herself in the kitchen. Leeanne leaned against the door frame and took a deep breath. She had to stop thinking about him. It wasn't as if they were friends or anything.

"Leeanne," Mrs. Thomas called, "the trays are ready to be set up."

She hurried off to the kitchen, glad to have something to do to occupy her mind. But it didn't work. Rolling silverware didn't require that much mental ability and she couldn't get Gabriel's face out of her mind. He'd seemed so, so . . .

"Leeanne, what're you doing?" Mrs. Thomas's voice cut into her thoughts.

"Huh?" Leeanne jumped, startled. She saw Mrs. Thomas gazing quizzically at the tray. "Oh, my mind wandered, I guess Jamie doesn't need three sets of silverware."

"You look like you've been doing some serious thinking," Mrs. Thomas said kindly. "Is this place getting to you?"

"Getting to me?" Leeanne repeated. Of course it was. It would get to anyone. Jeez, she'd just spent two hours scrubbing toilets and talking to people who'd be dead by Christmas. "You mean, is it depressing me?"

"Something like that." Mrs. Thomas turned

back toward the stove and lifted the lid on her spaghetti sauce. "You want to talk about it?"

Leeanne stared at Mrs. Thomas's back. In the three days she'd been here, she'd never seen the cook with anything except a cheerful smile on her face and a kind word for anyone who passed through the kitchen. "How do you keep it from getting to you?" she finally asked.

"I don't." Mrs. Thomas threw her an amused glance. "It gets to me, I mean, it would anyone. People come here to stay a few weeks or maybe a month or two before they die and you get attached to them. You get to like them and care about them and then you find yourself praying for a miracle because you don't want them to die." She turned and faced Leeanne. "But they die anyway. Course it bothers me. Especially when the young ones come in."

"You mean the ones like Gabriel?"

Mrs. Thomas's expression softened into a gentle smile. "He's special, that boy."

"How?"

"He's got so much to give to the world." Mrs. Thomas shook her head. "He's not like most young men. He's different. Sensitivelike, he doesn't look at the world the way most folks do, and I don't think it's just because he's facing something a boy his age shouldn't have to face. It don't seem fair that he's going to die. It'll be a heartbreak for me when he does."

"Then why do you do it?" Leeanne asked. "Why do you stay here?"

"It's my job."

Leeanne shook her head. "You work so hard and you're a great cook, you could get a job anywhere."

"Why thank you." Mrs. Thomas smiled, pleased at the compliment about her cooking. "You're more perceptive than I thought. Yes, I do it because I want to. I do it because someone's got to and it might as well be someone like me. At least I can give the patients here a little joy and comfort in their last days. That's what the Good Book tells us to do, so I do it."

"You're religious."

"Around a place like this," Mrs. Thomas replied, turning back to her sauce, "a little religion helps."

"I guess it does." Leeanne hated to admit it, even to herself, but she was curious about Gabriel. "Uh, how long does Gabriel have?"

"Two, maybe three months."

Leeanne tensed. "Exactly what does he have?" Polly had already told her, but one part of her wanted to hear it from someone else. "What's wrong with him?"

"A bad heart." She shook her head sadly. "The doctors tried everything. But it was no good."

"Couldn't he get a transplant or something?"

"No. The valves and the surrounding tissue were so damaged by the viral infection that a transplant's impossible."

Polly had told her that too, but Leeanne wondered if there was another reason he couldn't get a new heart. "Do they know that for sure? I mean, how do they know it wouldn't work? If it's a question of money . . ."

"It's not money," Mrs. Thomas interrupted, turning to look at Leeanne. "It's medicine. There isn't any reason to give him a transplant if it won't take. And it's such a shame. That boy's not just smart, he's talented too. A real artist. You should see his paintings."

Leeanne stared at the cook and resisted the urge to continue arguing that Gabriel should have a transplanted heart. Mrs. Thomas wasn't lying. You could tell by looking at her face that she was just as disturbed by the thought of Gabriel dying as Leeanne was. If there was no way, there was no way.

"He paints," she asked, "you mean pictures?"

"Uh-huh, and not just pictures. He did a whole wall once, down in L.A. A mural. There was a photograph of it in the paper." She broke off as Mrs. Meeker, the duty nurse, came into the kitchen searching for coffee. The two women started chatting, leaving Leeanne alone with her thoughts.

Leeanne finished the trays and stacked them on the utility cart. On the one hand, she thought as she pushed the cart through the empty hallway toward the elevator, she admired people like Mrs. Thomas, but on the other, she thought she was a little weird too. She couldn't imagine anyone actually *wanting* to work at this place. She couldn't understand why Mrs. Thomas hadn't run screaming into the night. She knew it wouldn't be much longer before she felt like screaming. These people were dying. This place was a house with no hope. Leeanne felt tears spring into her eyes as she remembered chatting with Jamie. Damn it, he was a nice man. He didn't deserve to die. He was only in his early forties. A few days ago that would have seemed ancient to her, but now it seemed pitifully young.

She felt a tear dribble down her chin. Annoyed, she wiped her face with her sleeve and pushed the utility cart into the elevator. Maybe acting depressed around her parents wasn't going to be all that much of an act after all.

The last tray was for Gabriel. Leeanne was loath to go back into his room, but she could hardly avoid it. He'd notice if he didn't get his dinner. She pulled his tray off the cart and knocked softly at his door.

"Come in," he called.

He was sitting up, the hospital bed having been raised to support his back. Leeanne took his tray over and placed it on the swinging counter, then she pushed the countertop in front of him.

Gabriel lifted the cover off his plate. "Spaghetti." He smacked his lips and dumped his silverware out of the napkin Leeanne had so painstakingly rolled. "No one makes spaghetti like Mrs. Thomas. She is one incredible cook."

"She is good," Leeanne agreed.

"Have you eaten her food?"

"I've snuck a taste a time or two. But you don't have to eat it to know it's great. The smell alone is enough to have me salivating." Leeanne realized she was hungry. Too bad she wasn't going to get any. Not that Mrs. Thomas would begrudge her a plate of spaghetti, but Leeanne didn't have time. She couldn't afford to miss the bus home. She started for the door and then noticed the book she'd seen yesterday still sitting on Gabriel's bookcase. "Can I borrow that?"

Gabriel looked up, his mouth full. He saw her pointing at the paperback, swallowed hastily, and nodded. "I thought you said you'd read that one?"

"I have," Leeanne said, snatching up the book before he could change his mind. "But I need to look through it again. I've got a book report due on Monday and the school library didn't have a copy."

"Why how very resourceful of you."

"And what does that mean?" Really, she didn't know why she let him get to her.

"Exactly what it says. You, of course, being the soul of honesty are going to report on a book you've already read. Boy, that should save you a lot of time," he sneered sarcastically.

"So what?" Jeez what a jerk! "It's not like I'm pinching the plot from Cliffs Notes. I *have* read it."

"Still sounds like cheating to me," he said, stuffing another bite of food into his face.

"Are you deaf or what? It's not cheating. I've read this damned book," she yelled.

"It is cheating," he argued. "The point of a book report is to read a book. Using one you've already read before defeats the whole purpose."

Leeanne couldn't believe what she was hearing.

What was he? The poster boy for the National Teachers Association? "Well, aren't you Mr. Holier Than Thou," she snapped, using one of her friend Jen's favorite clichés. "Don't tell me you've never done it before."

"Sure I did," he said. "I scammed a few book reports and a paper or two. You know what, though? I'm sorry now. It's one of the few things I regret."

That stopped her cold. "Why?"

" 'Cause easy ain't always better," he said cryptically. "You learn that the hard way when you're in my situation."

She stood and stared at him, not knowing what to say or even what he really meant.

Gabriel sighed and gave her an odd little smile. "It's okay, kid, I don't expect you to understand. Go ahead, take the book. I hope you get an A."

"Thanks," Leeanne mumbled. "I'll be back for your tray later."

He was asleep when she came back. Quietly she eased open the door and tiptoed into his room. His breathing was labored and heavy, his face pale. The bedside light shone directly onto his closed eyes but he slept on. Leeanne reached for the metal plate cover and then frowned as she saw three fourths of the spaghetti uneaten. She picked up the tray. Maybe she should say something to someone? He hadn't eaten much. Leeanne didn't know much about sick people, but she knew that they were supposed to eat and keep up their strength.

Closing his door, she eased the cart down the hall and onto the elevator. She ran into Mrs. Meeker downstairs. When she showed the woman Gabriel's plate and told her that he'd fallen asleep with his light on, the nurse nodded.

"Don't worry about him," Mrs. Meeker said. "I'll turn his light off and get him into bed when I do the night rounds."

"But he didn't eat much," Leeanne protested. She had no idea why she was worrying about Gabriel Mendoza. With the mouth he had, he was more than capable of taking care of himself.

Mrs. Meeker smiled sadly. "I know. He never does. Leeanne, a word of advice. These people are dying. All the food and rest in the world isn't going to stop it, so don't wear yourself out trying to save them. You can't. You'll worry yourself into an ulcer if you take it to heart too much."

"But how can you not worry about them?" she asked. Oh, what was wrong with her? Ten seconds ago she'd told herself that Gabriel could fend for himself, yet here she was worrying because he didn't eat his damned spaghetti. It wasn't like he'd thank her for her concern. But she couldn't seem to help herself.

"By doing the best you can," Mrs. Meeker said. "By making their lives as pleasant and comfortable as possible and being there for them. Even if all they want you to do is sit quietly by their beds. Sometimes that's all you can do."

*   *   *

Leeanne missed the seven o'clock bus and had to take the seven-twenty. Cursing under her breath, she climbed aboard and took the first empty seat available. She was going to be late for dinner. She was starving to death and it was getting dark outside. God, she had to be out of Lavender House before they went off daylight saving time. The thought of busing it home in the darkness was more than she could stand.

She dashed into a 7-Eleven store before going home. Arming herself with a bag of pretzels, some Twinkies, and a chocolate bar, she hurried home.

"Hi, Leeanne," her mother called from the dining room. "You're late."

Leeanne dropped her backpack onto the hall table and forced a sad, forlorn expression on her face. She found she didn't have to try hard to look miserable. All she had to do was think of Jamie and Gabriel.

She sat down at her spot at the dinner table. Her father looked up over his designer-frame glasses and smiled at her. "Hi, honey. How come you're so late?"

She fired her first shot. "I missed my bus. I was helping Mrs. Thomas wash some late dinner trays. Some of the patients are real slow, I mean, it takes them a long time to eat. I can't rush them. It wouldn't be fair. They're in such a, well . . . bad situation as it is."

Her mother looked at her father and then back at Leeanne. "Nevertheless, it's important that you get home on time," Eileen McNab said briskly.

"You've still got your homework to do tonight. Hurry up and eat."

Leeanne stared at the platter of chicken in the center of the table. Her mouth watered. Her nostrils twitched at the tempting smell. Pretzels and Twinkies, usually two of her favorite things, didn't have much appeal right at the moment. But by God, she wanted out of that place.

She fired her second shot. "Speaking of homework," she said, pushing her chair out and getting to her feet. "Maybe I should get started. I've got to study for a French test tomorrow."

"But you haven't eaten a bite," her mother protested. "I know your homework's important, but so is your health."

A shaft of guilt sliced through Leeanne. But she managed to push the ugly feeling to one side. Worrying her parents was exactly what she wanted, no needed, to do. "My health is fine. Believe me, working at Lavender House pounds that point home. It's just that I'm not hungry."

"You should be," Eileen said. "You didn't eat any breakfast this morning either and you only picked at your dinner last night." Her eyes narrowed thoughtfully. "You're not developing an eating disorder, are you?"

So she had noticed, Leeanne thought triumphantly. "I don't have anorexia," she said. The last thing she needed was her parents bugging her about that. "I just don't have much of an appetite."

"You've got to eat something," her father said, looking very concerned.

Leeanne shrugged faintly. "Dad, I'm not hungry and I've got a ton of homework and I'm really tired. I want to get some sleep tonight."

She could tell by the way her parents exchanged worried glances that she was starting to get to them. In another day or two, she'd have them just where she wanted them.

Once her father realized the horrible effect that place was having on his darling daughter, he'd move hell and earth to get her out of there.

Chapter
Four

September 22

Dear Diary,

I overslept again this morning, so I'm writing this on the bus bench. I don't know what's wrong with me. This morning I blew a perfect opportunity to escape Lavender House! Mom fixed me oatmeal with cinnamon. She hasn't done that since I was ten, so I know she must've been really, really worried about me. Anyway, there I was digging into my cereal when Dad walks in and flops down at the breakfast table. I couldn't believe it! He hasn't eaten breakfast with me in years. He starts in on how he and Mom might be busy, but that they loved me very much. They were real sorry I was stuck doing community service but they thought I should be made to take responsibility for my actions . . . etc. etc. Well, the upshot of it was they wanted to know what was bothering me.

And this is where I blew it big time. I put down my spoon, picked up my backpack, and told them nothing was WRONG. I actually said, "Oh, don't worry about me. I'm just getting used to a new schedule." Stuffing myself full of food wasn't such a hot move, either. They both looked very relieved. Dumb, huh. Now I'll never get out of that place. I can't believe how stupid I was.

My day went steadily downhill after that. At lunch, Jennifer told me that after the game on Friday night, Todd's taking her out to eat.

Leeanne frowned at the last line of her diary. She didn't know what to write next, which was a first for her. Normally, she didn't have any trouble pouring her feelings out. But the trouble was, she didn't *know* how she felt. Her life was too confused. She ought to be devastated by Jennifer's betrayal, but she wasn't. Mainly, she was irritated. She ought to be furious with herself for blowing a chance to get away from the house of the Living Death, but she wasn't. Oh, well, she thought as she glanced up and saw the bus coming, maybe I'm just getting used to it.

At the diner, Leeanne brightened considerably when she walked in and saw Nathan standing behind the counter. He was holding a Coke.

"Hi. I saw you get off the bus. I hope this is what you want," he said, waving the glass in her direction.

She was flattered. "It is."

They stared at each other for a moment, the silence a little awkward. Then they both spoke at once.

"Leeanne."

"Nathan."

Laughing, he said, "Ladies first."

"I was just going to ask you if you work every day?" Her own words surprised her. She was hardly playing it cool. But somehow, maybe it was because of the hospice, she didn't want to play games. She liked him. She wanted to know if he liked her, or if she was reading him all wrong and he was just being nice.

"Every day but Sunday," he said, his eyes gleaming with amusement.

Leeanne frowned at him. "What's so funny?" God, she'd die if he was laughing at her, if he'd realized she'd developed a crush on him.

"Nothing's funny," he said, "except that I was just getting ready to ask you the same thing."

"Every day but Sunday," she echoed, enormously relieved. She might want to be honest, but she hadn't relished the idea of him not taking her seriously.

He gaped at her. "You volunteer six days a week?" he asked incredulously. "God, what are you, a saint?"

Leeanne didn't know what to say. How did one explain tying up practically every moment of one's free time? She didn't want to tell him the real reason she was working at Lavender House. Not yet anyway. Not until they got to know each other a little better.

"I'm not exactly a saint," she said with a nonchalant shrug. "I'm just a regular person. But if you're going to do something, you should really commit to it, don't you think?"

"Well, yeah, but six days a week." He didn't look convinced.

Leeanne didn't want him to think she was weird. Maybe she should just tell him the real reason she was at Lavender House. But then he gave her a slow, admiring smile. She decided that wild horses wouldn't drag the truth out of her. No one had looked at her like that in her whole life.

"Well, it sounds a little crazy, but I think it's cool. You're right," he said. "Commitments are important."

"You work six days a week," she pointed out, suddenly uncomfortable. "That's even harder than doing volunteer work."

"Only because I have to," he said. "We need my paycheck to make it." He broke off and turned away. For a moment Leeanne thought he might be embarrassed, but when he swung around, he was holding a wet cloth. Without looking at her, he started wiping a nonexistent spot on the countertop. "Uh, how does your boyfriend feel about your volunteer schedule?"

"I'm not seeing anyone right now," she said, trying not to smile. His approach wasn't exactly subtle, but she thought it was kind of cute. "How does your girlfriend feel about your schedule?"

"I'm not seeing anyone now either. My girlfriend and I split up last June," he said, raising his gaze to meet hers. "Look, I'm not trying to come on to you or anything, but I really like you. You're pretty, you're smart, and I know you study hard. But most of all, I really admire the kind of person you are. Not every girl that has as much going for them as you do would spend their free time helping at a hospice."

"Oh, it's no big deal."

"Yes it is," he insisted. He paused and took a deep breath. "I'd like to ask you out but I don't have much free time and I don't have a car."

Stunned by his honesty, she stared at him. He liked her. He really, really liked her. "I'd like to go out with you," she said. "And I guess you could say I am pretty busy too."

A slow smile crossed his face. "I think we can work something out. We do have Sundays."

And I'm grounded, she thought. Frantically she tried to think of a way out of this mess. Why hadn't she told him the truth right away. Because he'd have thought you weren't such a saint. But he was getting ready to ask her for a date on Sunday! She had to tell him something.

"This may sound weird," he continued, not bothered by her silence. "But we could go to the library together. That's not exactly exciting . . ."

"That's fine," she said quickly. The library. Thank God he'd picked the one place her parents would let her go. "I know you've probably got to study."

"I've got a term paper due," he explained. "But it'll only take a couple of hours to do my research. We could go get some dinner afterward."

"Sounds great. I've got a book report due Monday. I can write it up while you're doing your research." Leeanne decided she'd worry about having dinner with him later. Now, she just wanted to make sure she got to spend some time with him.

"Like I said, I don't have a car. But I can pick you up. We could take the bus."

"No, don't bother. I'll meet you at the library. It'll be easier for both of us."

A customer came in and sat down at the end of the counter. Nathan nodded and started to walk away. "Is one o'clock okay?" he asked.

"Fine."

The customer was only the first of a rush. Leeanne didn't get another chance to talk to Nathan before she had to leave. She smiled and waved good-bye as he was carrying a huge order to one of the booths. He didn't wave back but the smile he gave her warmed her heart.

All the way to Lavender House, she mentally rehearsed the line she'd use on her folks. It ought to be a piece of cake. Even they couldn't object to her doing research. As for the dinner date, well, she'd cross that bridge on Sunday.

"This sure beats cleaning toilets," Leeanne said as she shoved the vacuum cleaner in the hall closet.

"Amen to that," Polly agreed with a laugh. Dressed in a skintight yellow jumpsuit, a black velvet collar around her neck, and a pair of four-inch-high sling-backed patent leather heels, she wasn't anyone's model for a hospice volunteer. But she and Leeanne had just spent the last two hours dusting and cleaning the common room. She discovered that despite her flamboyant appearance, Polly was amusing, kind, irreverent, and highly intelligent. She'd also found out that Polly volunteered here because she'd lost her only brother to AIDS. Leeanne hadn't known what to say, so she'd just mumbled that she was sorry. The words had sounded so lame. But Polly had smiled and thanked her.

"I don't know about you"—Polly lifted her arms over her head and stretched her spine—"but my back's about had it. I could use a rest. I think I'll go up and see if Jamie wants to play cards."

"You're pretty close to him, aren't you?" Leeanne asked. Though Polly had chattered cheerfully the whole time they'd worked together, she hadn't asked a lot of nosy questions. For that, Leeanne was grateful. But she was curious. She couldn't stop wondering why someone like Polly, who'd already lost someone she cared about to AIDS, could spend so much of her free time with a man who'd soon be dead from the same disease that had killed Polly's brother. How could she do it?

"Jamie's a doll." Polly brushed a piece of lint off her shoulder. "And I like to think that if I hadn't been there for Jim at the end, someone else would have. It's kinda like I'm, I don't know, paying off a debt. I was lucky that I got to be with Jim when he was dying. But there are so many that have no one to come and see them, or hold their hands, or even just talk to. And I suppose Jamie and I've gotten close because we're the same generation. Both of us can remember the Cuban Missile Crisis and Howdy Doody." At Leeanne's puzzled expression, she laughed. "Before your time, kiddo. Anyway, we seem to have a lot to talk about. Besides, he's a joy to know."

"Better than some around here," Leeanne mumbled. She threw a quick glare toward the back. Gabriel, a book in his hands, had gone out to the garden half an hour earlier. On his way past, he'd tossed her a casual, "Hello, Princess Leeanne. Glad you could make it."

Polly threw back her head and laughed. "Don't be so sensitive. Gabe's a nice kid. Believe it or not, he watches for you from the window. But don't tell him I told you. He'd come unglued."

"Yeah. He's probably waiting to pour a bucket of water over my head," Leeanne said. But she was secretly pleased. There was something about Gabriel that made her . . . she couldn't put her finger on it, but she knew he could get to her faster than anyone else she'd ever met.

"Why don't you go out and spend some time with him before it gets too dark," Polly suggested as she headed for the stairs.

"Don't we have more cleaning to do?" Leeanne didn't want to risk running foul of Mrs. Drake. The director was still watching her like she thought Leeanne was going to steal the silver.

Polly stopped and turned. "No. We're through with chores for the day. Part of our job is to spend time with the patients. That's the main reason we're here. Like I said, a lot of these people don't have anyone to visit them."

"Uh, okay." Leeanne hovered by the closet door. She decided she'd wait until Polly went upstairs and then she'd go find someone else to visit with. Maybe Mr. Kemper wanted to play cards.

But she didn't. Instead, she found herself moving slowly toward the French doors that opened off the back parlor. On the terrace, she stopped and scanned the area.

The garden was protected by a twelve-foot-high stone wall. A flagstone terrace went down two steps to an emerald-green lawn. The perimeter of the fence was lined with flower beds of daisies, impatiens, roses, and tangled vines of ivy and some other clinging plant Leeanne couldn't identify. In the center of the lawn stood a huge oak tree with a picnic table and benches nestled below. Gabriel was sitting on one of the benches. He was watching her.

Leeanne stepped across the terrace and walked toward him. She didn't really want to see him, but she felt she had to. One of the reasons she'd overslept this morning was because of something he'd said. Now she needed to ask him a favor.

"Hi," she said.

"Hi." He looked off to his right. "Don't you love it?"

She glanced in the direction of his eyes. "Love what? The wall?"

"No, you dummy. The colors. The colors of twilight."

"All I can see is that it's getting dark. Look, Gabriel, about what you said yesterday . . ."

"Forget what I said," he interrupted impatiently. "Take another look. This time, look until you really see."

"See what?"

"Humor me," he snapped, "I'm a dying boy. Just open your eyes and concentrate."

Leeanne clamped her mouth shut, took a deep breath, and stared around the garden. The shadows had lengthened with the setting sun; the air was calm and smelled of cut grass and roses. She took a deep, calming breath letting the sweet evening scents fill her lungs.

But she didn't see any colors. Maybe his illness or his medication had addled his brain?

She felt his hand on her wrist and he tugged her down beside him.

"Keep staring, keep looking," he whispered in her ear. "You won't see bright colors. You'll only see the pale muted hues of the fading light. But they are spectacular. There's two or three different colors of lavender alone."

As he spoke, she suddenly understood. It was still daylight, but it did look different. The lawn appeared darker and richer, like a carpet of deep rolling velvet, the hanging vines formed spiky intricate patterns against the lightness of the stone wall, and the tree above her head rustled gently in the wind. She stared, really seeing the twilight for the first time. Gabriel was right. There were colors. Pale, ghostly, but delicately beautiful in the fading daylight. The sharp shadows against the stone wall, the deepening color of the new mowed lawn, the lavender shades of shadow hovering faintly outside the line of her vision. It was lovely. And it was the first time she'd ever noticed it.

"Feel it," Gabriel said softly.

She sighed as a deep sense of peace washed over her. The fading light seemed to soften the whole garden, making it for a moment almost a mystical place. From far off, she heard the song of a bird. Without realizing it, Leeanne held her breath and a slow smile curved her lips.

Gabriel laughed softly. "You do see the difference, don't you?"

"I never noticed it before," Leeanne whispered, not wanting to break the magic of the moment with loud voices. "It's so beautiful. And the birds, I'd forgotten how birds sound."

"Twilight's not the best time for listening. Wait until spring, the night birds sing then."

"Night birds?" She stared at him suspiciously, wondering if he was making fun of her. "What kind of night birds?"

"Who knows what kind of birds they are. All I know is sometimes they sing loud enough to keep you awake half the night. I can remember dropping into bed at two A.M., exhausted from studying, and those damned birds would start up like a blasted mariachi band. It used to drive me nuts. Then I got to like it."

"I've never heard them."

Gabriel shrugged. "You must be deaf then, they sing loud enough to bring you out of a coma. Did you come out here for a reason?"

That brought her back to reality quick enough. She frowned. "As a matter of fact, I did."

"You gonna tell me or are we gonna play twenty questions?"

"If you'll wait just a moment, I'll tell you. Honestly, do you have to be so damned rude?"

"It's a gift." He grinned. "Okay, kid. Sorry. Let's start over." Gabriel sobered and cleared his throat. "What can I do for you, Princess Leeanne."

She rolled her eyes. "For starters, you can knock that off."

"Your wish is my command."

She ignored his sarcasm. She needed a favor. Him and his damned nagging yesterday had pricked her conscience. But she wasn't about to tell him that. "I need to borrow another book."

His eyes widened in surprise. "You got another book report due?"

"No, it's the same one," she admitted reluctantly. "But your rudeness really bugged me. It kept me awake half the night." Damn, she thought, what was wrong with her? Every time she opened her mouth around this kid she was saying exactly what she didn't want to say.

"I'm flattered." He puffed out his chest arrogantly. "Obviously, I have a much greater effect on you than I realized."

"Don't let it go to your head," she said. "Considering the emotional roller coaster I've been on since I got busted, Bart Simpson could have an effect on me."

"Conscience bothered you, huh?" he said smugly.

"Don't be dumb," she said loftily. "My conscience is perfectly clear. I merely thought about what you said and decided that for once, you were right. Reporting on a book I've already read would be cheating. Besides, like I said, I'm really confused these days. That's all."

He gazed at her for a moment. "Yeah, I can see how that might happen. You pull off a dumb prank and get busted for it and the next thing you know, everyone's acting like you're a thief. Must have got to you, huh?"

She nodded. That was exactly how she felt. "I guess when you said reporting on a book I'd already read was cheating, well, that was just a little too close to . . ."

"Stealing," he finished, his tone unexpectedly sympathetic.

Leeanne nodded again, too embarrassed to speak.

"Okay," he said, his tone brisk. "What do you want to borrow?"

"Do you have anymore SF?"

"Does the pope have holy water?" He got up. Leeanne noticed he had to use the top of the picnic table to steady himself. She wondered if she should try to help him and then instinctively decided against it. He'd probably smack her if she touched him.

"Come on," he ordered gruffly, "let's go look in my bookcase."

It took a good ten minutes to get to Gabriel's room. He collapsed on the bed, his breathing hard and labored, as soon as they walked inside. He didn't look good. This time, she didn't care if she offended his masculine pride. "Are you okay?" she asked.

"Of course I'm not okay," he rasped, coughing. "If I was okay I wouldn't be here." He gestured at the bookcase. "Take a look. I'm going to rest a minute."

She studied him for a moment, noted the determined set of his jaw, and then turned away. There was a call button right beside his bed; if he needed help, Leeanne hoped he'd ring for the nurse. There wasn't much she could do. The thought made her feel about as useful as a kindergartner. Hell, she thought, kneeling down in front of the bookcase, I don't even know how to do CPR. For the first time in her life, she wished she'd taken the CPR class at the Y. What if he was having a heart attack?

The titles of the books were a vague blur, she was concentrating so hard on listening to Gabriel breathe she couldn't tell an Asimov from a *Star Trek* novel. After a few moments, she heard him sigh and his breathing slowed. Finally, it seemed to return to normal.

Leeanne sagged in relief. She spotted a book by John Wyndham, one of her favorite authors, which she hadn't read. Grabbing it, she rose. "Can I borrow this?"

He nodded. "But make sure I get that one back."

"You like Wyndham?"

"Would he be in my bookcase if I didn't?" Gabriel sank back against the pillows. "Who else do you like?"

"Just about anyone except Heinlein or the fantasy authors."

"Fantasy sucks," Gabriel agreed, "but I like Heinlein. Have you ever read *Stranger in a Strange Land*?"

She made a face. "It didn't punch my buttons. I thought it was kinda boring."

"Are you kidding?" He was incensed. "That's one of the greatest SF books ever written. It's a classic, like the *Foundation* trilogy or Dune series."

"Get real," she sneered. "They shouldn't even be mentioned in the same breath." Within seconds, Leeanne was sitting on Gabe's bed having one of those wonderful arguments that only a true book lover could understand.

For the next half hour they compared, argued, and discussed dozens of different books and authors. They didn't stop talking till Polly came in with Gabriel's dinner tray.

"We're running late tonight," Polly apologized

as she put Gabe's food down. "Mrs. Thomas couldn't get her biscuits to bake."

Leeanne glanced at her watch. "Jeez, it's five past seven."

"Time does fly when you're having a good time," Polly chirped.

"Leeanne wasn't having a good time," Gabriel smirked. "She was getting her butt whipped in an argument."

"In your dreams, buster," Leeanne sneered. "We'll continue this tomorrow. I'm going to miss my bus if I don't get going."

But the truth was, Leeanne had had a good time.

Saturday she worked her tail off and even if Gabriel had been up and about, she wouldn't have had time to talk to him.

Mrs. Drake kept her busy from the minute she arrived until she was putting on her jacket to go home.

Both her parents were in a good mood when she walked into the living room. Leeanne judged that the time was right to see what she could do about having dinner with Nathan on Sunday.

It was surprisingly easy, they didn't question her much when she announced she'd be going to the library on Sunday afternoon and would probably stay until it closed. As long as she didn't run into anyone she knew while they were at dinner, she was home safe.

Leeanne spent the rest of Saturday night reading the Wyndham book and finished it on Sunday morning. The hours crawled by. Her parents left at eleven-thirty for the country club. At eleven thirty-two she dressed for her date with Nathan.

It took her over an hour to decide what to wear.

Nathan was sitting outside when she arrived a few minutes past one. "Hi," he said, getting up from the stone bench he'd been sitting on. He wore a pair of tight, faded jeans that fit him like a second skin and a blue work shirt with the sleeves rolled up.

"I'm sorry I'm late," she said, "but the bus was a few minutes off."

"That's okay." He grinned. "I just got here myself. You want to go on in and get started?"

For the next two hours they both pretended to concentrate on their studies. But Leeanne noticed that every time she glanced up, he was staring at her and she knew she was equally guilty of peeking at him out of the corner of her eye whenever she thought she could get away with it. Lucky for her she was good at writing reports, as being this close to Nathan didn't do much for her powers of concentration.

"Are you about finished?" Nathan whispered in her ear.

She nodded, glanced at her watch, and saw that it was close to three-thirty. The library closed at five. She'd have almost two hours with him before she had to be home!

"Do you want to eat now," Nathan asked when

they were outside, "or do you want to go for a walk or something?"

"Why don't we walk over to the coffee shop on Fifth and Edinger? I really have to be home by five-thirty."

"Sounds good to me." He took her hand.

They talked easily as they walked. By the time they arrived at the restaurant, Leeanne was convinced he was the most wonderful boy she'd ever, ever gone out with.

Leeanne ordered a burger platter and Nathan ordered fish. "I get enough burgers at Henry's," he said with a grin. "Sometimes I dream I'm drowning in a vat of cooking oil."

She laughed. "How long have you worked there?"

"Four years. I started when I was a sophomore in high school." He reached for his coffee. "After my dad died, I had to help support my mom."

"That must have been hard." Leeanne hadn't ever met anyone her age who *had* to work. "I mean, if you were working, you probably didn't have much time for a social life."

"You do what you gotta do. I just had to get organized with my time," Nathan said. "It messed up any extracurricular activities, but I can't say that I missed much. I've made a lot of good friends at Henry's."

"Is that where you met your girlfriend?" The question slipped out before she could stop it. Leeanne silently cringed.

"Hardly. Gina wouldn't be caught dead eating in

a greasy spoon like Henry's." Nathan smiled. "I met her in senior English. We went steady for a year before she realized I wasn't a nice preppie boy who was playing around with a part-time job to keep himself busy."

Leeanne picked up a french fry. "She didn't like you working?"

"It wasn't just my job," he said casually, "it was me. I was Gina's rebellion against her parents. I didn't know it at the time. Hell, I thought her parents approved of me. She told me they admired the fact that I was helping to support my mom. But she was lying. They didn't approve of me or my background. One day, she grew up. She got over her rebellious stage and she got over me real fast too."

"I'm sorry," Leeanne mumbled.

"Don't be. It wasn't like I was in love with her." He grinned again. "More like I was in lust with her. But the whole experience taught me something important about relationships."

She tensed. "What?"

Nathan looked directly into her eyes. "Anything built on lies can't last."

Chapter
Five

September 24

Dear Diary,

Mom and Dad still aren't home so I'm snatching a few minutes to write. I'm in a bind here—I really like Nathan but I hate letting him think I'm something I'm not. Maybe I should tell him the truth about why I'm at Lavender House. But then again, maybe I shouldn't. But I don't want him to think I was lying—I mean, I'm not really lying just because I haven't explained my personal business. Am I? Oh, who am I kidding. Lying by omission is still lying. But I really, really like him. Next to Nathan, Todd looks like a little boy. Not that Todd isn't a nice guy, he is. But the closest he's ever come to work was crewing on his cousin's yacht. Maybe I'll wait until Nathan and I get to know each other a little better before I tell him the truth. Why is life so complicated? I finally meet a guy who's just incredible, and I end up in a mess.

"Leeanne," her mother yelled from downstairs, "we're home. Come on down. Your father wants to talk to you."

Leeanne's brows drew together. That sounded ominous. She shoved her diary in her drawer and hurried downstairs.

"Hi, how was the country club?" she said as she came into the living room. Her father was standing in front of the fireplace, her mother sitting on the sofa.

"The country club was fine," her father replied. "How was the library?"

Oh, God, Leeanne thought, they've found out I snuck out and had dinner with Nathan. "Uh, it was fine. I got my book report finished and I got some research done for my history paper." She cringed inwardly. Even though she was telling the truth, the words sounded like a lie.

"Good." He stepped over and sat down on the sofa next to his wife. "Your mother and I would like to talk to you."

"What about?" Leeanne asked warily.

"About this place you're working at, this Lavender House." He paused. "Leeanne, it's not a nursing home. Joe Martell is on their board of directors. He said the place is a hospice."

She decided to play dumb. "So?"

"So! Is that all you have to say," her mother

said. "You're working at a hospice and you don't even bother to tell us."

"I didn't think it was important. I mean, there isn't really much difference between a nursing home and a hospice."

"Not much difference!" Her mother shook her head. "Don't be ridiculous. People go to hospices to die."

"People die in nursing homes too."

"And a lot of them don't," Mrs. McNab snapped. "You're seventeen years old. The probation people had no right to put you in a place like that. It could be horribly detrimental to your emotional health."

She decided to try a different tactic. "You're acting like I'm at fault here," she said defensively. "If you'll remember, a few days ago you and Dad seemed to think that I deserved whatever I got. Why are you making such a big deal of it now?"

Her parents exchanged guilty glances.

"However it may have seemed to you at the time," her father finally said, "let me assure you that had I known Lavender House was a hospice and not a nursing home, I'd have done my best to make the Probation Department reassign you."

"You were with me when it happened," Leeanne pointed out.

"Oh, let's not discuss what's already been done," Eileen said quickly. "The point is a hospice is no place for a seventeen-year-old girl."

"But, Mom." Leeanne fought to keep her voice level. "I like working there."

"I don't care if you like it." Her mother leapt up from the sofa and began to pace the room. "Being constantly exposed to death at your age is very unhealthy. Why, just look at what it's done to you."

"It hasn't done anything to me."

"Yes it has." She stopped in front of the fireplace, whirled around, and frowned at her daughter. "Just look at you. You're not eating properly, you're depressed, and God knows what kind of diseases you're exposed to at that place."

Leeanne swallowed heavily. Damn, this was her own fault. If she hadn't spent all that time faking depression, neither of her parents would have given a hoot about what Lavender House was. Well, maybe without the theatrics they wouldn't have come so unglued once they heard what it was. Now she had to do some serious damage control.

"I'll admit I was a little down at first," Leeanne began carefully, "but that was just because I was so upset at being arrested. It had nothing to do with the hospice."

"Do they have AIDS patients there?" her father asked, staring her directly in the eyes.

Leeanne didn't dare lie. It was too easy to check. "A couple. But I don't have all that much to do with them."

"How much is 'that much'?"

"I don't even see them that often," Leeanne said honestly. "They're usually sleeping when I get there."

"Do you have any contact with their bodily fluids?"

She sighed. Daddy was going to act like a lawyer now. "Not really." This time she did fib. Of course it wasn't really a lie. Scrubbing a few toilets and sinks didn't constitute contact with body fluids. And she didn't want her community service switched to someplace else. Besides, she knew if she left Lavender House she'd never see Nathan or Polly or Gabriel again. "Look, all I do is help set up the dinner trays, do a little light housekeeping, and visit with some of the patients. There's one or two AIDS cases there and both of them are so sick, they spend most of their time in bed."

"But it's still a hospice," her mother yelled. "And I don't think you ought to be there. It's not right. It's not healthy."

"Calm down, dear," her father murmured. "Everything will be fine. If it looks as if the place is affecting Leeanne's emotional health, I'll take care of it. I do have some connections in the legal community in this town."

"And what does that mean?" Leeanne asked.

"It means that we might be able to get your community service moved over to Community Hospital." He watched her face as he spoke.

"But I don't want to work there," she said. "Community has plenty of volunteers. Every teenybopping airhead at Landsdale High works there so they can flirt with the interns. Community needs another candy striper like I need another hole in my head."

"But that's not the issue," her mother interjected.

"You seem very committed to staying at Lavender House," her father said thoughtfully. "Why?"

Leeanne was desperate to make her parents understand. "Because for the first time in years I feel like I'm doing something worthwhile, something other than just worrying about myself. I may only fold towels and fix dinner trays and read to people, but that's all those patients have," she argued. "Community service should mean paying back what you owe. Lavender House really needs me. I'm useful. I'm doing something other than worrying about how popular I am and whether or not my grades are good enough to get me into a good college."

"At your age," her father said dryly, "I should think worrying about your grades would be important."

"Not to the exclusion of life," Leeanne shot back. She was amazed she actually had the nerve to argue with her dad. But this was important to her, more important than she'd realized. The thought of never seeing her friends again made her almost sick to her stomach. "And, Dad," she continued, trying another tactic, "I like working at Lavender House. Nobody's died since I've been there."

"All right, all right." He held up his hand for silence. "I'm not saying I'm going to do anything right away."

"But, Gerald," his wife said.

"Hear me out, Eileen," he continued calmly. "This is the first time I've ever heard our daughter make a passionate plea for something other than a new pair of shoes or a trip to Palm Springs with her friends. I'm impressed."

"Thanks, Dad."

"Don't thank me yet. Because I do feel it would be in your best interests if I make some inquiries. And if I see this place is affecting your emotional health, I'll have you out of there so fast it will make your head spin. Does that sound fair?"

Inquiries? About what? But Leeanne was too relieved by the reprieve she'd just gotten to push him any further. "Sounds fair to me." She smiled at both of them. Her mother, arms folded across her chest, still looked like she'd like to spit nails, but her father grinned back at her.

"Well, I don't like it," Eileen mumbled. "I don't like it at all. A hospice is no place for a seventeen-year-old girl."

Leeanne worried all night. The thought of never seeing Nathan or her other friends again filled her with dread. And she was determined it wasn't going to happen. No matter what it took she was committed to staying at Lavender House. They needed her. Even in the short time she'd been there, she'd noticed the lack of volunteers and visitors.

At breakfast on Monday morning she pigged out on cereal and toast and made sure both her parents saw it. She smiled cheerfully till her cheeks ached and chattered like a bluejay in her mother's ear on the drive to school. She'd make them realize Lavender House wasn't depressing her even if it killed her.

At school, she pushed her troubles to the back of her mind and concentrated on her studies. If her grades slipped, her parents would use that as an excuse to get her moved. She even went so far as to spend her lunch period in the library, getting some of her homework done. She read her English assignment on the bus ride across town.

Nathan was standing with her Coke in his hand when she walked into the diner. "Hi. How's it going?"

"Fine," she lied, forcing herself to smile. "Did you get your paper done?"

He nodded and then peered at her closely. "Are you okay? You look a little worried."

Amazed, she stared at him. "How did you know? I came in grinning like a fiend."

He laughed. "Your face might have been smiling but your eyes weren't. What's up?"

She silently debated the wisdom of telling him the truth. "Oh, it's just my folks," she said, taking a quick sip of the Coke. "They're not so thrilled with me spending so much time volunteering at the hospice."

"Maybe they have a point."

Leeanne looked up sharply. "Hey, you're supposed to be on my side. Remember?"

"I am on your side," he said. "But let's face it, you do spend a lot of time there. Maybe your parents are uptight about your grades slipping?"

"My grades are fine." Leeanne was getting more

and more depressed by the minute. Didn't he realize that if she didn't come to Lavender House every day, she wouldn't see him. But of course he didn't realize that, she thought. How could he? She hadn't exactly told him the truth. He didn't know she was grounded. He didn't know she was doing community service and that if she wasn't at Lavender House she'd be spending just as many hours tied up somewhere else. And with her luck, she'd probably be assigned to pick up trash in Hargraves Park! Damn.

"Then what's their problem?" Nathan asked.

"My emotional health." She smiled faintly. "They think it isn't good for me to be around people who are dying."

"Oh, yeah, well, I kinda see their point." He reached behind him and picked up a wet dishcloth. "How do you stand it?"

"No one's died since I've been there," she admitted. Leeanne wasn't certain how she would handle the situation, but she didn't think she'd fall apart. People died all the time.

"Order ready," the cook yelled. Nathan grinned and went to pick up the food.

They didn't have time to talk much after that. Leeanne finished her Coke, waved good-bye, and left.

Mrs. Drake was sitting behind the desk when she walked into the hospice. She was so absorbed in her work she didn't look up when Leeanne entered. Leeanne had to clear her throat to get the woman's attention.

"Oh." Startled, Mrs. Drake gave her a quick grin. "Hi. I didn't hear the door open."

"You look like you're working hard on something." Leeanne shifted her backpack to the floor.

"The flyer."

"Flyer?"

"For our open house." She shook her head and pulled off her glasses. "We have one every year and every year I haven't got the faintest idea what to say to get the community to come visit us. Some of us just aren't very talented with words . . . or drawing or anything else that gets people not to dump the flyer in the trash before they've even read it."

"Why do you have an open house?" Leeanne asked. Surely having a bunch of people all over the place would upset the patients and cause all kinds of problems.

"To raise money," Mrs. Drake said bluntly. "This place doesn't run on air and good wishes."

"But I thought . . ." She paused, not sure what she'd thought.

"What? That we had government funds." Mrs. Drake smiled cynically and shook her head. "No way. We're funded by private donations, churches, community groups, and anyone else who cares about the plight of the dying."

"Oh, sorry, I didn't realize."

"Don't be sorry, just tell me you know how to draw," Mrs. Drake pleaded. "Please, we need something snappy on this thing, something to catch people's eyes and keep them from dumping it into the nearest trash can."

"Sorry again." Leeanne laughed at the director's crestfallen expression. "I do windows, but I can't draw worth beans."

"Why don't you have Gabriel design it for you?" Mrs. Thomas came round the corner carrying a tray of coffee. "He's such a talented young man, I'm sure he'd love to come up with something absolutely beautiful for the flyer. Maybe he could do a bird or a rainbow or a picture of the tree in the backyard."

"That's a wonderful idea." Mrs. Drake looked like she was going to kiss Mrs. Thomas. "Why didn't I think of that?"

Leeanne's mind was working furiously. An open house. It might be the answer to her prayers. If she could get her parents to come, to actually see this place, maybe they wouldn't worry about her. "Uh, when is it?"

"October fourteenth," Mrs. Drake replied. "So be sure and tell all your friends. We want as many people here as we can get."

"Just make sure they bring their checkbooks," Mrs. Thomas said dryly.

They laughed. Then Mrs. Drake handed Leeanne her duty roster for the rest of the week. Leeanne didn't think it looked all that bad. She only had to clean bathrooms once.

Today she was assigned to visiting with patients and meal trays. She put her backpack away and hurried upstairs.

She knocked softly on Gabriel's door. "Come in," he bellowed.

She grinned. He must be having a good day. She stepped inside and then came to a dead stop. Gabriel was sitting in front of the window, an easel in front of him. "Close the door," he muttered, not looking up from his painting.

She eased the door shut and craned her neck to get a look at what he was working on. He glanced over at her. "Well, don't stand there getting a crick in your neck, come on over and tell me what you think."

She was ridiculously flattered. Leeanne crossed the room and stood behind him. She gasped. The painting was exquisite.

"It's a blackbird," she murmured. "And Twin Oaks Boulevard." Of all the things she'd expected, this surprised her the most. He'd captured the bird sitting on a telephone wire above the bus stop across the street. The black feathers reflected the glare of the sun setting behind the liquor store, the sky was the color of twilight, and the way the bird was poised made you think the animal was just about to take off in flight. He'd captured the feeling of the city streets—the coming darkness softening the grimness of the bars on the houses and the setting sun casting a velvety blur over the potholed street and littered sidewalks. It was bizarre and strange and should have made her sad. But it didn't. It made her feel alive.

"Well," he demanded, glaring at the painting like he expected it to argue with him. "What do you think? And don't give me that line that you don't know anything about art but you know what you like. Just tell me the truth."

"It's beautiful."

Gabriel turned his head and saw that she was staring at the painting. He heard the awe in her voice.

"For a little rich girl," he said, "you've got good taste."

"Modest as well, I see," she muttered.

He put his brush down and she stepped back. Gabriel stood up and stretched. Leeanne winced. He was so thin, she could practically count his ribs through the material of his T-shirt.

"How'd you like the book?" he asked as he strolled over toward the bed.

Leeanne wasn't fooled for a minute. She could see he was exhausted and trying hard not to let it show. Males! They all tried hard to act so macho. "I loved it. Wyndham's a great writer, better than Asimov."

It was like waving a red flag in front of a bull. Gabriel launched into a heated defense of his favorite author and the debate was on.

"Besides," Gabriel insisted a good half hour later, "Asimov is responsible for the concept of the positronic brain, a concept, I might add, that's been ripped off by every movie or TV show with robots. Just look at Data on *Star Trek*—"

"Data's an android," Leeanne corrected. "Not a robot."

"Details, details, android or robot, it's still

Asimov's concept." He paused. "Hey, you want to see some SF art?"

"Sure," she said, not sure what he was talking about, but not about to let him know it.

He nodded toward the closet. "You'll have to get it. Pull out the big envelope from the top shelf."

Curious, she did as she was told. The envelope was one of those huge mailers. As she handed it to him, she noticed how pale he was. "Uh, are you sure you're up to this? I can come back tomorrow if you're getting tired."

"I'm okay," he said brusquely, but Leeanne knew he was lying. He struggled to get the flap open and then pulled out a stack of drawings. Handing them to Leeanne, he said, "Take them over to the desk so you can lay them out flat."

Leeanne was amazed. The first drawing was a landscape of another world or maybe another dimension. Crystals, exquisitely drawn and detailed, sprouted out of alien soil. Among the sparkling jewels, humanoid beings of light and shadow wandered. Excited, she turned the drawing over and went on to the next one. They were all superb. Beautiful, exotic, and completely alien. She whirled around, wanting to thank him for sharing this with her.

He was sound asleep.

Leeanne stacked the drawings neatly and tiptoed out of the room. As she shut the door, she gave him one last guilty glance. She shouldn't have visited so long. She had to remember that he was a very sick person.

Leeanne ran smack into Mrs. Drake. "Oh, hi. I was just on my way downstairs to start the dinner trays."

"No rush," Mrs. Drake replied. "Were you visiting with Gabriel?"

"Yeah, he was showing me some of his artwork." Leeanne saw that the director had the half-finished flyer in her hand. "But then he fell asleep."

"I won't disturb him then," she said. She started to turn and then suddenly swung back around to face Leeanne. "You've been spending a lot of time with Gabe, haven't you?"

"Sure," she said, puzzled by the question. "Isn't that all right? I mean, isn't that one of the reasons I'm here?"

"Don't look so worried, of course it's okay. I'm glad that Gabe gets to spend some time with a young person. He needs friends right now."

Leeanne hesitated. "Don't any of his other friends ever come to visit?" It wasn't really any of her business, but she was wildly curious.

Mrs. Drake pursed her lips and shook her head. "They can't handle it. So they stay away. He occasionally gets a letter or a card from one of his old buddies, but that's about it."

"How awful," she said.

"Not really," Mrs. Drake said briskly. "Death scares most people. And Gabriel is dying. Even his girlfriend doesn't come around anymore."

"Girlfriend?" Leeanne got a funny feeling in her stomach. "I didn't know he had one."

"He doesn't now." Mrs. Drake sighed. "But he

did when he first arrived. Poor Gabe, he was pretty crazy about her too. But as he got weaker and weaker, she just stopped coming around."

"What was her name?" Leeanne knew she was being nosy. Gabriel should be the one telling her this. But she couldn't help herself.

"I don't remember, I think it was Karen or Connie or something like that." Mrs. Drake gazed at Leeanne, studying her silently. "Look, I'm glad you and Gabe have some kind of friendship going, God knows, the poor kid needs something. But I don't want you to forget something very important."

"What?" Leeanne stared at her warily. If Mrs. Drake was going to give her the speech about her and Gabriel being from totally different backgrounds, she could save her breath. Her interest in Gabriel Mendoza was strictly platonic.

"Gabriel's dying."

"I know that," Leeanne said.

"Do you?" Mrs. Drake smiled sadly. "I wonder."

"Well of course I do," Leeanne insisted, "this is a hospice."

"That's right. And there won't be any heart transplants or miracle cures. Gabriel will be gone soon. I just wanted you to understand that." She turned and started down the hall.

"Mrs. Drake," Leeanne called softly. "How long does he have?" She knew she'd asked this question before, but maybe, just maybe this time she'd hear an answer she liked better.

The director stopped but didn't turn around. "We don't know. A week, a month, two months.

Some things, Leeanne, are simply in the hands of God."

Leeanne pushed Mrs. Drake's words to the back of her mind. No sense on dwelling on something she couldn't change, she told herself as she rooted around in the back of her closet for an old box of books. Her fingers shoved aside a pair of tennis shoes and brushed against cardboard. She pulled the box out and flipped open the flaps.

She grinned, she hadn't seen her old collection of science fiction since last summer. Leeanne yanked the books out, looking for something she could take to Gabriel. She tossed aside two books by Philip K. Dick, half a dozen *Star Trek* novelizations, and some vintage Harrison until she spotted what she wanted.

The phone rang. Leeanne scrambled to her feet and grabbed the receiver. "Hello."

"Uh, hi, Leeanne, it's Nathan."

"Nathan, hi." Be cool, Leeanne, be cool. You don't want to scare him off.

"We didn't get much time to talk today," he continued. "And I wondered how things were going?"

"Things are fine." She blew a strand of hair off her face. "Though I'm a little covered in dust right now. I pulled some old books out from my closet." God, that sure sounded lame. "I, uh, thought I'd take them over to Lavender House."

"What kind?"

"What kind of what?"

"Books. What kind of books are they?"

"Science fiction." She waited for him to sneer.

"Got any Robert Heinlein?" he asked excitedly.

Leeanne grinned. Thank God, Nathan liked to read. "No. I don't like him all that much. But I've got some Harrison and Asimov and lots of others, I'll bring them by the diner before I take them to the hospice. You can go through them and pick out what you want. When you're through with them, I'll take them to Lavender House, okay?"

"Sounds good. How are you going to get them there? You're not planning on dragging a box of books on the bus, are you?"

Leeanne's smile faded. "I was going to ask my mom to give me a lift. She's not working tomorrow." That was the truth, Leeanne had planned on getting her mother to take her and the box of books. It was all part of her campaign to get her parents to back off from trying to get her reassigned.

"How about I pick you up?" he suggested. "I've got my mom's car tomorrow. I could pick you up at school and give you a lift."

Leeanne panicked. She wanted to say yes more than anything else in the world, but she didn't want him near anyone that knew she'd been arrested and was doing community service. Her dear friend Jennifer wasn't above letting the cat out of the bag.

"But if we do that," she pointed out, "I'd have to drag the books to school tomorrow. The box is too big to fit into my locker."

"We can run by your house and pick them up," he suggested.

Now she really panicked. Damn. She just knew if he came to the house her mother would blow it. "Thanks just the same," she said, "but Mom really wants to see Lavender House. She's never been there."

"Okay," he said. "So I guess I won't see you at the diner tomorrow?"

"You will. You want to go through the books, don't you?"

He laughed. "Good. I like seeing you every day." He paused. "Uh, are you busy Saturday night?"

"Well, uh," she hesitated. God, he was going to ask her out and she was still grounded! But there had to be a way. She racked her brain, trying to remember if her mother had mentioned that she and Dad were going out. "No, not really."

"Would you like to go to the movies?" Nathan asked.

Leeanne took a deep breath. There had to be a way. She'd find a way even if it killed her. Maybe her parents would take pity on her and let her off restriction. If she said no, Nathan might never ask her out again. "I'd love to."

"Great. Do you like foreign films?"

"I've never seen one," she admitted. "No, wait a minute, I watched a French movie on cable last week. Why?"

"Well, there's a double feature playing at the Art Cinema in Ventura, I thought maybe you'd like to go see it. It's two French movies . . . I'm, uh, kinda into foreign films," he said cautiously. "But if that doesn't sound like fun, we can go to something else."

It sounded like heaven to her. She'd sit through a documentary on the life cycle of ferns if it meant she could be with Nathan. "The French movies sound good. I'd like to try it."

They chatted for a while longer and then hung up. Leeanne stared at the phone for a moment, trying to decide the best way to approach her folks.

It rang again. Startled, she jumped. This time it was Jennifer.

For ten minutes she listened to Jen babble on about cheerleading practice and Todd. "It's too bad you're still grounded," Jennifer said, not sounding in the least sympathetic. "There's a party at Todd's house Saturday night."

"That's okay," Leeanne replied. "I've got other plans."

"Oh, you mean you're allowed out?"

"Not exactly, but I'm hoping to talk them into letting me off for good behavior for a few hours."

"Oh." Jennifer paused. "Then I guess if you've got plans you wouldn't be interested in coming to Todd's place."

Leeanne couldn't see Nathan wanting to socialize with an airhead like Jennifer. "Thanks all the same, but I'm busy."

"Doing what?" she asked suspiciously.

Leeanne knew that Jen didn't believe her. She

probably thought she was going to be sitting home watching TV. "I've got a date."

"With who?"

"His name's Nathan."

"Nathan," Jennifer mumbled. "I don't know anyone named Nathan."

"Why should you?" Leeanne asked. "He goes to college and Saturday night he's taking me to the Art Cinema in Ventura."

"The Art Cinema," Jennifer yelped. "You mean that place that shows all those weird movies?"

"Not weird, foreign. I'm going to see some French films."

"Yuk."

"How do you know it's yuk?" Leeanne asked. "Have you ever seen one?" She knew it was stupid to argue with Jennifer. She'd die before she'd ever admit she was wrong. Leeanne suddenly realized how little she and Jennifer had in common anymore. The revelation was shocking. On top of that, she suddenly understood that in all the years they'd been friends, they'd also been competitors. If she got a B on a test, Jennifer made damned sure that she made an A the next time around. If Leeanne bought a new dress, Jennifer made sure she got a whole outfit. Even Todd. Jen hadn't been all that interested in Todd until he'd asked Leeanne out. And she hadn't understood it until now. How could she have continued a friendship with someone that she didn't really even like all that much and who obviously didn't like her either. It was crazy.

"Well, no," Jennifer admitted reluctantly. "But you don't have to experience something to know you wouldn't like it. I don't have to jump off a cliff to know I wouldn't like hang gliding either."

Chapter Six

September 30

Dear Diary,

Boy, did I luck out. Mom and Dad were so touched by my dedication to my community service that they practically fell all over themselves letting me go out tonight. That was kind of a sticky situation too. I mean, I didn't want Nathan coming here to the house because I was afraid the folks would let it slip about my getting busted. So, after some quick thinking and some fancy footwork on my part, I'm having him pick me up at the library. What the heck, I am going to swing by the library—I need to drop some books off. Anyway, this week has gone okay. No rumblings from Dad about getting me moved out of Lavender House and I even got him and Mom to agree to come to the open house on the fourteenth.

Gabriel is still being a royal pain, he teases

me constantly but I'm getting to the point where I don't even mind it all that much. Yesterday he drug me outside to help him feed the birds.

Leeanne's pen paused and a slow smile curved her lips as she remembered yesterday afternoon. She'd arrived at Lavender House cranky and fighting a sinus headache. The Santa Anas, those bone dry hot winds which swept in from the desert were blowing fiercely. Gabriel, holding a portable stereo in one hand and a bag of crumbled bread in the other, had met her at the foot of the stairs, ordered her to follow him and led her outside.

"What's up," Leeanne asked, as they came out onto the patio.

"We're going to feed the birds," he replied, slipping a tape in the stereo and tossing her the bag of bread crumbs. "You'll love it, Princess. It's one of life's freebies."

She made a face at him but he only laughed as the strains of Mozart filled the air. Leaves flung by the wind danced in heady circles around the garden. Leeanne thought Gabriel had gone nuts. But she did as he asked.

For half an hour they listened to classical music and tossed bread crumbs to the birds as the wind whipped around them. The tree branches and palm fronds seemed to move in time to the music spilling from Gabe's stereo.

It was wonderful, it was magical and Leeanne's bad temper and headache evaporated. She wasn't certain why she'd enjoyed the experience so much.

Maybe because it was the first time she'd ever taken the time to watch birds or maybe it was because Gabriel's enthusiasm for life's simple pleasures was so intense. She didn't know and she didn't care. She only knew she'd never feel the hot Santa Anas on her skin again without thinking of how good it felt to be alive.

She glanced at her watch, saw that it was time to get moving, and put her diary back in the bedside drawer. Taking one last look at herself in the mirror, she decided the neatly tailored olive-green slacks coupled with her ivory blouse was absolutely perfect. The colors looked good on her and the outfit showed off her figure. She hoped Nathan would be impressed.

At the library, Leeanne shoved her books in the book drop and then pulled her hairbrush out of her purse for a quick repair. She'd just popped it back in when she spotted Nathan walking up the steps. He grinned appreciatively when he saw her. "You sure take your schoolwork seriously," he said, nodding to the folder tucked under her arm.

"I just want to get it out of the way," she replied. "I hate having things hanging over me."

"Yeah," he agreed. He reached for her hand and entwined his fingers with hers. "Me too. I was up at the crack of dawn studying this morning. I've got a big test on Monday. The car's over here."

They crossed the street toward an older model, red Toyota. Nathan pulled out a set of keys and unlocked the door on her side. "It's not exactly a Rolls, but it'll get us there."

Leeanne slid into the front seat and then leaned across and unlocked his door. She didn't care what kind of car he drove, just being with him was enough. She frowned, wondering if she should say something along those lines. But she didn't want to come on too strong, she didn't want him to think she was desperate.

"I hope you like these movies," he said as he twisted the key in the ignition. "They've both had good reviews, but they'll be in French with English subtitles. That doesn't bother you, does it?"

"Subtitles? No."

"Good." He smiled. "They drive some people crazy. My mom hates them."

Leeanne couldn't think of a thing to say. Talking about school would be a mistake, he could care less about what went on at Landsdale High. They had no friends in common, so that topic was out, and she didn't want to ask him any questions about himself, because then he'd probably start asking her questions and she didn't want to have to lie anymore. Darn. This was getting complicated. Why don't you just act naturally, her conscience whispered.

She didn't dare. She'd die before she let him know she was only at Lavender House because she was doing community service. He liked her. He really liked her and she wasn't prepared to spoil his good opinion of her. Not yet, anyhow. Maybe after they got to know each other better she could risk it. But not now.

"You're awfully quiet tonight," Nathan said.

"You're not exactly a chatterbox yourself," she replied.

"I guess we're both a little uptight." He glanced at her. "First date and all. It's a drag, isn't it?"

"What? Going out with me?"

"Nah." He looked at her. "That isn't what I meant."

She laughed. "I know. Besides, this isn't our first date. We went to the library together and had dinner."

"That doesn't count," he replied. "It wasn't at night. Now I guess we've got to go through the rituals. Will she like the movie? Will she expect me to kiss her good night? You know, all the stuff that goes along with being with someone you like."

Leeanne stared at his profile for a moment and burst out laughing. Good grief, Nathan had just admitted he was as nervous as she was. "I think you're right. First dates are a drag. So why don't we pretend we've done this dozens of times before and not worry about it?"

"Sounds okay to me," he said, grinning from ear to ear.

The tension evaporated and they talked easily all the way to the art cinema. To her surprise, Leeanne enjoyed the films.

It was past eleven before they left the theater. Yawning, Leeanne leaned back against the seat of the car and watched Nathan out of the corner of her eye. "The movies were great."

He pulled around the corner and stopped at a

red light. "Yeah, I liked them too. Are you busy tomorrow?"

She desperately wanted to see him again, but she didn't want to press her luck. She couldn't see her parents letting her out two days in a row. "I've got to study."

He frowned in disappointment. "I should study too," he mumbled. "But I'd rather spend the day with you."

"But I was planning on doing it at the library."

He slanted her a glance. "Funny, that's where I was going to study. Maybe we can share a table." He reached over and turned on the radio. Soft rock music filled the car and Leeanne closed her eyes.

Neither of them felt the need to talk. But this time, the silence wasn't awkward or strained. It was smooth and calm and very, very natural.

"Open your eyes, sleepyhead," Nathan said twenty minutes later, "we're almost home."

Leeanne blinked in surprise. She was so relaxed she'd fallen asleep. "Oh, God, I'm sorry. I didn't mean to conk out on you."

"Don't worry about it. You'd better give me directions to your house," he said.

"I left my car at the library," she replied.

He gave her a funny look but said nothing.

"It's the white compact over there." She pointed to her car that was parked right under a streetlight by the library steps.

Nathan pulled up behind it. He turned the engine off and turned to her. For a long moment he just stared at her. Leeanne would have given six months clothing allowance to know what he was thinking. "I had a wonderful time tonight," she murmured.

"So did I," he said softly. "Leeanne, I really like you."

"I really like you too." Leeanne had the feeling he was leading up to something.

"But I don't want to get involved if there's a problem."

Stunned, she stared at him. "There's no problem, Nathan. I don't know what you're talking about."

"Okay, I'll just say it straight. Is there some reason you don't want me to see where you live or meet your parents? Tomorrow's the third time we'll see each other and I still don't have the faintest idea what your address is . . ."

"Nathan, that's crazy, I had to use the car to get to the library," she protested. "My address is 246 Hollander Road."

"Are you sure that's all there is to it?"

"Of course I'm sure. What else could there be?"

He drummed his fingers on the steering wheel and stared straight ahead. "I don't know. Maybe you don't want your folks to know you're seeing me. It was like that at first with Gina. When we started dating I always had to pick her up away from her house. When I finally confronted her, she admitted I wasn't the kind she usually dated. Nice girls like her didn't go out with working stiffs like me that smelled of cooking oil and hamburger grease."

"But I thought you said Gina used you to rebel against her parents."

"She did, but she played some mind games with me first. Wouldn't go anywhere with me where we might be seen by any of her rich friends, wouldn't meet my mom." He shook his head and smiled cynically. "I was such a jerk. It took me weeks to realize what she was up to. Look, I'm not trying to push you into anything, but I want to make it real clear right now. I'm not ashamed of where I come from or what I am. If that's a problem for you, maybe we'd better stop seeing each other before one of us gets hurt."

She leaned over and touched his arm. "Nathan, I want to keep on seeing you. Believe me, your background isn't a problem for me. I think you're terrific. You're smart, you're helping to support your mother, you work hard, and I think you're gorgeous."

He turned toward her, a smile on his lips. "Okay, but is it going to be a problem for your parents?" He slipped his arms around her waist as he spoke.

"No, my folks will love you," she said. And it was the truth. Her parents, both from working-class backgrounds themselves, respected hard work and education more than anything.

He pulled her closer and brushed his lips against hers. Her heart slammed into overdrive and her blood pressure skyrocketed. Nathan drew back, stared into her eyes, and then kissed her completely. A moment later he let her go and opened the front door. "Come on," he ordered, tugging her out of the car. "Let's get you safely to your car. Do you want me to follow you home?"

Leeanne, still reeling from his kiss, couldn't think very fast. "Uh," she started to say no, then changed her mind. "Yes, I think I'd like that."

For the next couple of weeks, Leeanne felt like she was walking a tightrope. She continued to see Nathan whenever she could and managed somehow to convince him she wasn't ashamed of him or his background. It was a tricky job too, she thought as she stared morosely out of the diner window.

The Santa Anas had long gone and with them the warm days of summer. A hard cold rain fell, splattering the panes of glass with water and flooding the streets.

"Want another Coke?" Nathan asked.

"No, I've got to get to the hospice." She started to pack up her backpack.

"Leeanne, how come you don't drive your car?"

She shrugged. She'd been waiting for him to ask that question and she was ready for it. "It's cheaper to take the bus, gas costs money."

"Yeah, even though it's Mom's car, I pay my share 'cause I use it a lot. The sucker still costs me a bundle to run," he agreed. "Are you all ready for tomorrow night?"

She nodded and jerked her head toward the window. "We're ready, I just hope the weather is. I'd hate to see people not show up for the open house just because of the rain."

"Don't worry so much," he said. "There'll be plenty of people there. Even my mom's coming."

Leeanne smiled. She approved of the way he spoke about his mother. Her own mother had once told her that you could tell how a man really felt about women by watching how he treated his own mother. Leeanne hoped that was true. "My parents are coming too," she said, turning to give him a wide smile. "And I can't wait to introduce you to them."

"Ditto," he said softly. He dragged his eyes from her as the front door opened and a customer walked in, struggling with an umbrella. Leeanne decided she'd better make tracks.

She arrived at the hospice wet and breathless. Polly was at the front desk. "Hi, kiddo. How ya doin'? Lord, it's not fit for ducks outside."

"Hi, Polly, let's just hope it lets up before the open house." She put her backpack and umbrella on the floor and started to unsnap her jacket. "What's on the roster for tonight?"

"Nothing." Polly giggled. "Believe it or not, the place is clean enough to eat off the floors, Mrs. Thomas is refusing to let anyone in the kitchen because she's whipping up some surprise goodies for tomorrow, and Mrs. Drake is upstairs taking a nap."

"So what am I supposed to do?"

"Keep your jacket on and come on up," Gabriel's voice called from the top of the stairs.

Suspicious, Leeanne flicked a wary glance up.

Polly laughed again. "Oh, don't be so paranoid. Go on up and see what he wants."

She snorted. "Humph, the last time I did that he enticed me into a poker game and I lost two weeks worth of allowance."

"Come on, chicken. I promise, no poker games," Gabe shouted from upstairs.

"Oh, all right, let me put my stuff away."

Leeanne hurried off to stash her pack and umbrella. Her relationship with Gabriel was weird. Real weird. He still called her a princess and gave her a hard time, but she gave back as good as she got and she noticed he was always hanging around the front when she came in. She smiled wryly as she started up the stairs. Heck, she'd even come in last Sunday to bring him another box of books and a batch of homemade chocolate-chip cookies. What she hadn't told him was that she'd stayed up half the night Saturday baking the darned things. She didn't want him to get a swelled head. Between the hospice, Nathan, homework, school, and Gabriel, she'd practically forgotten what her old friends even looked like.

"Come on, get the lead out," he called.

"What's the rush," she complained. "It's not like we've got to be somewhere."

"Yes we do," he corrected, giving her an evil grin as she came up the last few stairs. "It might stop." He turned and led the way down the hall.

"What might stop?"

"The rain."

"Gabriel," Leeanne said patiently as she followed him. "You've got it wrong again. We want it to stop. We're having an open house here tomorrow night and we don't want all our nice rich guests to get their checkbooks wet, do we?"

He laughed as he pulled open a narrow door at the end of the hall. "Don't worry, princess. They'll take one look at me and the other pathetic inhabitants of this joint and the money will flow like water through a sieve."

Leeanne's mouth opened in surprise, but she couldn't see his face to tell if he was joking or not. He'd already started up a narrow flight of stairs. "Come on, slow poke. You're going to miss it."

"Miss what?" she asked warily as she climbed the stairs and came up into the attic. Gabriel was in a funny mood today. That crack about "pathetic inhabitants" was telling.

He stood at a window, his back to her. Silently he motioned her over. "Come look."

Leeanne moved closer. She stared out the window and from the top of the four-story house, it was a fabulous view. Or it would have been if it wasn't shrouded in darkness. "At what?"

"Twin Oaks Boulevard," he whispered. "Go on, take a look, a good look. See all that neon down there."

"Yes."

"Now look at the street, see how the colors split and pool and reflect in a dozen different ways?"

She bent her head toward the window, her nose touching the cool glass, and stared hard at the street below. Going south from the hospice, there were half a dozen or more neon signs. The screaming red of Hanrahan's Bar and Grill, the blaring yellow of Ernestine's Checks Cashed, the blue and white stripes of The All Night, All Right Quick Mart, and the brilliant green Li Li's Chinese Restaurant. They all blended on the rainy street into a mass of floating streams of color. Leeanne stared and stared, she couldn't believe this was the first time in her entire life she'd ever noticed how gorgeous reflected neon in the rain was. "It's wonderful," she said softly. "It makes that sleazy street look magical . . ." She broke off as she realized how hokey she sounded. But Gabriel didn't laugh.

She flicked him a quick glance and saw his gaze locked on to the street too. His eyes glittered and a soft smile curved his cheeks. In the faint light of the attic, she noticed how gaunt his face was, his skin seemed stretched tightly over bones, his mouth bracketed in lines of pain.

"Gabriel," she said softly. "Are you all right?"

"No," he admitted. He didn't turn and look at her and she was glad. "I'm not ever going to be all right."

"Maybe you should go lie down." She blinked rapidly because she could feel her eyes start to smart with unshed tears.

"Not yet," he said fiercely, though he didn't raise his voice. "This might be the last time. I want to see it all, I want to sear it onto my brain so I'll never forget."

She knew what he was talking about. Biting her

lip, she turned and stared out the window herself. A tear streaked down her cheek and she let it fall. Damn. He thought this might be the last time he ever saw rain. Leeanne pushed the thought out of her mind and swallowed heavily. She wouldn't let him see her cry; she wouldn't let him know how bad she felt for him. Gabriel didn't appreciate pity.

"Hey, princess," he murmured in her ear, "don't let it get to you. I didn't bring you up here to make you cry. I wanted someone to share the beauty with, that's all."

She swiped at another escaping tear. "Even if it was me?" She tried to say the words lightly, hoping he'd snap back at her with something to make her angry or make her laugh.

But he completely ruined it.

Gabriel put his arm around her shoulder and pulled her close. Leeanne burst into tears. She couldn't have stopped if someone had put a gun to her head. Sobs wrenched from deep inside her exploded into the quiet room. Gabe swung her around and cradled her against his chest. He didn't try to soothe her; he didn't murmur meaningless platitudes that everything would be all right. He simply let her cry.

Finally, the storm passed. Embarrassed, Leeanne pulled away and stared at her shoe. "Sorry," she mumbled. "I don't know what came over me."

He took her hand. "Let's go down to my room," he said, "I think we need to talk."

Gabriel didn't say a word till they were safely in

his room with the door shut. "Have a seat, princess."

"Gabe," she began, "look, I didn't mean to come unglued up there, but . . . but . . ."

"It finally hit you, didn't it?"

Mutely, she nodded. It had finally hit her. He was going to die. He wasn't going to be around to aggravate her, and tease her and debate with her and show her the wonderful things she'd never taken the time to notice before. And damn it, she was going to miss him. "Yeah, I guess it did."

He smiled wearily. "It used to hit me that way too."

"Used to?"

"Sure. When I was first diagnosed, I kept thinking it was all a bad dream, that one day I'd wake up and I'd find everything was okay." He walked over and sat down next to her on the bed. "But that ain't the way things are, princess. And believe it or not, accepting it makes it a helluva lot easier to handle."

"But how can you accept it?" She was suddenly enraged. At him, at the universe, at life, at everything. "You're so talented. You've got so much to give. You're a brilliant artist! You're smart, you could contribute so much to this world."

"You mean why me and not some poor slob with nothing going for him?" Gabriel looked amused.

"That's exactly what I mean," she snapped, "it seems to me there are a lot of mean, nasty selfish people in this world who don't do anything but take up space. Some of them live to be a hundred and they don't contribute anything but pain and misery . . ."

He stopped her tirade by gently placing his fingers over her lips. "Don't, princess. One thing I have learned is that none of us are fit to judge what others give to this world." He dropped his fingers and leaned over and gently kissed her on the lips.

Leeanne was stunned. She kissed him back.

They drew apart and stared at each other. Gabriel broke the silence first. "I shouldn't have done that," he said. "But I've wanted to kiss you for a long time. Since the first time I saw you."

"I'm sort of going with someone," she admitted reluctantly, "and I shouldn't have kissed you back."

"Don't panic, princess. It was only a friendly kiss."

"Do you still think about your girlfriend?" Leeanne wished she could take the words back as soon as they slipped out.

But Gabriel didn't seem to mind her question. "Connie? Sure I do. I was crazy about her."

"How could she do it to you, Gabe?" Leeanne clenched her hands into fists. "How could she walk out on a guy who's . . ."

"Dying," he finished.

Leeanne looked down at the floor, embarrassed by her outburst. This was none of her business. She had no right to pry into his past, into what was probably a painful and miserable experience. Getting dumped wasn't nice when you were healthy, it must be ten times worse when you were facing the Grim Reaper. "I'm sorry."

"Don't be. I'd like to tell you about her. Once she stopped coming around no one ever mentioned her to me again," he sighed. "Guess they thought they were being kind. But the fact is, not talking about her made me feel really lousy. It was like we hadn't even existed as a couple. I want to talk about Connie. I understand why she stopped coming. She couldn't handle it."

"*She* couldn't handle it," Leeanne said dully. "But what about you? You needed her."

"And she was there for me when I needed her," he said gently.

Leeanne felt a surge of sick emotion rip through her gut. But she didn't understand what she felt.

"Connie isn't a bad person," he continued, "she genuinely loved me. When my mom died, Connie was there for me. She was there for me when I was diagnosed, when I went for all those lousy treatments that didn't do anything but make me sick, and she was there for me when I knew I had to come here."

"But she isn't here now." Leeanne murmured.

"She couldn't take it anymore," he said. There was no bitterness or anger in his voice. Only acceptance. "The last time I saw her, she told me she couldn't stand to watch me die. You see, I'd accepted what was going to happen. She couldn't. Poor Connie. She'd handled so much already, I told her she didn't have to."

Leeanne simply didn't understand.

He grinned and swung his legs onto the bed and leaned back against the headboard. "So tell me about this boyfriend of yours."

"You'll get to meet him tomorrow night. He works at the diner up on the corner and he's coming to the Open House."

"You mean Nathan?"

"You know him?"

"Sure, he sometimes brings in pies or cakes from the restaurant. He's a nice guy. Plays a mean hand of poker too." Gabriel shook his head. "Man, that's hard to believe. You and someone like Nathan."

"What do you mean by that?"

"Just that you're kinda from different worlds."

Leeanne rolled her eyes. "Lots of couples are from different backgrounds. That doesn't mean they can't have a relationship."

"Hey, don't get so defensive. I didn't mean you should break up with him or anything. You're not going to turn on the waterworks again, are you?"

"No," she snapped. "I'm not going to turn on the waterworks as you so delicately put it."

"Good. So tell me, how long have you been seeing each other?"

"We met right after I started working here."

"Have you introduced him to your parents?"

"Well, not exactly . . ." She broke off at his knowing look. "And it's not what you're thinking either."

"How do you know what I'm thinking?" he taunted. "You're not exactly a mind reader."

"It doesn't take a mind reader to see through that sneer," Leeanne sputtered. But she wondered what he really meant by that remark. "The only reason I haven't introduced them to Nathan is because I don't want him to know I got busted. My parents would be bound to let it slip."

That did surprise him. "You're joking, right?"

She shook her head. "I wish I were. The truth is, I'm kinda up the creek on this one and I don't know what to do about it." She wanted his advice. Leeanne realized that she trusted Gabriel more than any friend she'd ever had. She didn't know how she knew she could trust him, it wasn't something she could put her finger on. But she knew all the way down to the marrow of her bones that he was a friend who wouldn't betray her confidence or her trust.

So she told him everything.

Gabriel listened carefully, his face impassive as she spilled her guts. It never occurred to her that he had bigger problems than she did. She had a feeling that Gabe would slug her if she tried to stop now. Hearing her troubles put them on an equal footing. They were friends. Friends shared the good as well as the bad.

"So let me see if I have this right," he said when she'd finished. "He thinks you're working here out of the goodness of your heart, right?"

"Right."

"And tomorrow night he's going to meet your folks."

"Right. And I'm terrified they might accidentally blow it."

"Them blow it," Gabriel said incredulously. "Are you crazy? You'll be lucky if someone from Lavender House doesn't let it slip. We're not exactly bursting with volunteers, you know. It's quite possible Polly or Mrs. Thomas or someone else might say that they hope the Probation Department sends us a dozen more just like you."

Leeanne moaned. "I hadn't thought of that. God, what am I going to do?"

"Well, I'm not into giving people advice."

She snorted.

"But," he continued, "in your case I'll make an exception."

"That's big of you. Oh, tell me, most wise one, what should I, a lowly mortal, do to get my butt out of this situation."

Gabriel grinned. "Tell him the truth yourself."

Chapter
Seven

October 14

Dear Diary,

I'm as jumpy as a freshman on the first day of high school. Tonight's the open house and if my parents don't like what they see, they'll have me out of there so fast I won't know what hit me. I've got my fingers crossed that everything will go right. I don't know what to do about Nathan. Gabriel gave me the lecture about honesty being the best policy, but he's not the one who'll pay if things go wrong. I will. Nathan's got this real hang-up about honesty and about being used. Plus, he thinks I'm a saint. Okay, I'll admit it, maybe I'm a tad shallow. But just a tad. I mean, I really do like the community service, I'm crazy about Nathan, and I'm not a bleeding heart do-gooder who's afraid to get her hands dirty.

Still, I felt kind of bad when I got home last

night. I mean, one minute I was bawling my eyes out because I felt so awful for Gabriel and the next I'm pouring out my troubles. What does that make me?

Leeanne sighed as she reread the diary entry she'd made that morning. Maybe if she did nothing, said nothing, things would work out fine. After all, she thought, as she stuffed her diary in the drawer, there was a good chance no one would say anything to Nathan about her reasons for being at the hospice.

"Does everyone understand?" Mrs. Drake asked the group of volunteers. "If you see any of our patients getting tired or nervous, let Mrs. Meeker know or help them upstairs yourselves and into their rooms. Jamie and Mr. Slocum are both feeling bad, so they won't be down at all."

"Is it okay for people to go upstairs?" Polly asked.

"They can go up and look at the common rooms, but the patients' rooms are off-limits unless that patient has invited someone inside. We're not going to violate anyone's privacy just because we're having an open house."

"Uh, what do we do if someone wants to make a donation?" Leeanne asked. She was hoping her own parents would crack open their checkbook, but she didn't think it likely.

Mrs. Drake grinned. "You hand them a pen and

tell them their check is tax deductible. Come on, don't look so grim. This is supposed to be fun."

But an hour later, Leeanne still wasn't amused. The house was filling up fast. She put down a tray of cheese and crackers, took a quick look around to see if her parents or Nathan had arrived, and then hurried back to the kitchen. Poor Mrs. Thomas was having fits, the food was disappearing faster than water down a drainpipe.

"Do you think we'll have enough?" Leeanne asked anxiously as she stared at the trays still waiting to be taken out to the dining room.

"We should," Mrs. Thomas replied, but she looked doubtful. She glanced up as Gabriel stuck his head inside.

Gabriel called to Leeanne, "Come on, princess, get your fanny moving. We've got a room full of hungry people in the parlor."

"I'm moving as fast as I can," Leeanne said, picking up a tray of stuffed celery. She hurried over to where he stood by the door. "How many more have shown up?"

"Well, all the volunteers are out there and most of their friends and family. A bunch of people from city hall showed up, after all, it is an election year. And at least half the freeloaders from in front of the liquor store are here." He grinned at Leeanne's gasp. "Don't look so spooked, kid, it's a good crowd."

"We're not going to have enough food," Leeanne wailed.

"Sure you will," Gabriel said. "Just tell the choir

from the Bethany Baptist Church they can't eat anything until they sing every known verse of 'Amazing Grace.' "

"That's not funny, Gabriel," Mrs. Thomas called from the other end of the kitchen. "If we run out of food, people will get cranky and cranky people don't write checks."

"I'd better get out there," Leeanne muttered. She swallowed and took a deep breath. Her parents would be here any minute. Nathan and his mother would be here soon too and she still hadn't decided what to do.

"Are you going to tell him the truth?" Gabriel asked quietly.

She shook her head and pushed past him. "I don't know."

Gabriel was right on her heels as she dodged small groups of people blocking her way to the dining table. "Honesty is the best policy," he nagged.

"Give it a rest," she hissed back. Then she smiled quickly as she saw Polly. Her friend had really pulled out all the stops for tonight. She wore a blue satin sheath dress with a scooped neck and long sleeves, matching satin shoes with four-inch heels, her hair was done up in an enormous mass of curls, and a pair of the longest rhinestone earrings Leeanne had ever seen dangled from her ears. By comparison, her own red silk sheath looked positively demure.

"Hey, you two, are you having fun?" Polly took Gabriel's arm, pulled him closer, and planted a kiss on his cheek.

Leeanne stared at the two of them. Gabriel looked good tonight. He wore a black corduroy jacket over a long-sleeved white dress shirt, no tie, and a pair of corduroy slacks. Unless you looked carefully, his clothes successfully masked his thin frame. His color was good and his eyes were clear and bright. But, Leeanne reminded herself, she'd keep an eye on him. She didn't want him getting tired. "I can't believe how many people showed up."

Polly laughed. "We've been really lucky this year. Let's hope this bunch feels generous and isn't just here for the food."

"Speaking of which," Leeanne said, "maybe I'd better circulate." She picked up a tray of food, put her best smile on her face, and headed into the crowd.

As she went from group to group, she kept her eye on the front door. Mrs. Thomas, Polly, and even Mrs. Drake were all doing their best to see that the guests were having a good time. The French doors had been opened onto the patio and a light breeze kept the crowded room from getting too hot. Above the chatter and laughter, soft music filled the air.

"Hey, princess." Gabriel materialized at her elbow. "Your boyfriend just walked in."

"Oh, no." Leeanne whirled and saw Nathan and a dark-haired, middle-aged woman standing in front of the reception area chatting with Mrs. Drake. Nathan looked over and spotted her. He grinned and waved, took his mother's arm and led her across the room.

"Hi, Leeanne. I'd like you to meet my mom, Susan Lourie." He introduced the two of them.

"I'm so happy to meet you, dear," Mrs. Lourie said, giving Leeanne a warm smile. "Nathan has told me so much about you. I think it's just wonderful that you give up so much of your free time to volunteer here."

"I'm pleased to meet you too," Leeanne replied. Her stomach was in knots. Great, now Nathan's mother thought she was a saint too. "And, uh, actually, I enjoy working here."

"Well, I'm certainly glad to hear that," a familiar voice said from behind her.

Leeanne whirled around. "Dad, Mom. You made it!"

"Of course we did," her mother said. She smiled at Mrs. Lourie and Nathan. Leeanne hastily introduced them.

"Mrs. Thomas needs you," Polly said. She'd appeared from nowhere at her elbow. Her mother's eyes widened at Polly's outfit and Leeanne bit back a smile. She introduced Polly to everyone and fled to the kitchen.

When she came out ten minutes later with another bowl of punch, she was pleased to see Polly chatting with her mom like they were old friends. Nathan and his mother were talking to her father and no one showed any signs of leaving.

She carefully lowered the punch bowl to the table. Gabriel was there, stuffing vegetables into his mouth like this was his last meal. "How's it going?" she asked.

He crunched a carrot stick. "I'm having a pretty good time." He tossed a quick glance over his shoulder at Nathan. "He's a nice guy. You can tell by the way he watches out for his mom. Too bad he's got a girlfriend who's playing games."

It was like rubbing salt into an open wound. "Knock it off, will you? I feel guilty enough as it is."

"Then tell him the truth."

"I can't." Jeez, she thought, Gabriel's really being pushy about this. Why?

"Why not?" he challenged. "You were quick enough to let me know your opinion of Connie yesterday, but at least she didn't lie to me."

She glared at him, but he didn't even blink. Darn. Why didn't she just tell Nathan everything? Because she was a coward? Because she didn't want him to think she was a jerk? Because she was afraid he'd never want to go out with her again? Leeanne didn't like any of the thoughts rushing through her mind.

"Darn," she muttered. Here she was talking to someone who was facing death and she couldn't even face telling her boyfriend the truth? "All right," she said slowly. "I'll tell him."

Gabriel simply stared at her, his eyes hooded and mysterious.

"Well," Leeanne prompted. She wanted a little credit here for what she was about to do. "Say something."

He smiled then. "By the truth, you shall be free."

"Yeah, right," she muttered, disappointed with him because he didn't seem to really understand what she was risking. "That and a buck will buy you a cup of coffee."

"What do you want? A medal or something? All you're doing is telling the guy the truth."

"That's easy for you to say."

"Don't be so negative." Gabriel laughed. "What's the worst that could happen?"

"You don't understand. Once he knows he might not like me anymore."

"If he doesn't like you for you," Gabriel said seriously, "then is he really worth having in the first place?"

"I like him," she hissed, totally exasperated. "I don't want to lose him."

"Again, what's the worst that could happen?" Gabriel reached for another carrot stick. "If the guy really likes you, then he'll take it okay. Otherwise, you're better off knowing now."

"He could dump me," she said. "That's what could happen. Then where would I be?"

"Where you always were," he said enigmatically. "Alive and kicking and able to make your own choices." With that, he turned on his heel and stalked off.

Leeanne felt like going after him, but she didn't. What would be the point? What did Gabriel expect of her? It wasn't his romance that might get shot down the tubes. It wasn't his life they were playing with here. And why was he angry? She was going to do the right thing; she was going to tell Nathan the truth.

"We need more napkins," Mrs. Drake called to her from the other side of the buffet table. Lee-anne nodded and hurried back to the kitchen. Between keeping the food trays stocked, circulating with the guests, and keeping her eye on their patients, she was too busy to worry about Gabriel's funny mood.

After putting out the last of the food, Leeanne dashed over to the French doors to snatch a breath of fresh air. She took a deep breath, bringing the sweet night air deep into her lungs. She heard a noise, like a foot scuffling on pavement, and peeked outside. Gabriel was standing at the edge of the terrace, his gaze on the sky. Leeanne looked over her shoulder. Nathan and his mother were in one corner chatting with her father; Polly and Mrs. Thomas were sitting on the couch having what looked like a real heart-to-heart with her mother. It looked like she could slip away without anyone noticing. She stepped outside.

He heard her coming up behind him. "Sorry, princess," he said, "I didn't mean to be so rough on you earlier."

"Then why were you?" she asked, more curious than angry now.

Gabriel shrugged. "Who knows? Sometimes I just get in funny moods." He turned and glanced at her, his expression stark in the moonlight. "Maybe I don't know myself."

A dozen different questions flew into her mind, but before she could ask any of them, the musical notes of a night bird filled the air.

"Gabriel."

"Shh . . ." He held a finger up to his lips. "Listen," he whispered. "The night birds are singing." He held his hand out and she took it. His fingers were slender, his flesh cool to the touch. But she didn't say anything. She didn't ask how he was feeling or why his skin was so cold or anything; she just stood there with him in the moonlight. He tugged her closer, dropped her hand, and slipped his arm around her shoulders. She leaned her head against him and closed her eyes. They stood together, listening to the night birds sing. Leeanne tried to swallow the hard lump that had suddenly lodged in her throat.

The birdsong increased in volume as several other birds joined in the chorus. Gabriel squeezed her shoulder and she felt tears well up in her eyes. Frantically she batted her eyelids, not wanting to spoil this precious moment with tears of sadness or pity. Moonlight cast the yard in pale flickers of light and shadow, the scent of jasmine filled the air. The birds sang.

Gabriel was dying.

Leeanne trembled, overwhelmed by the sudden, strange beauty of this impossible moment. A moment that once gone could never be recaptured. A moment stolen out of time. Leeanne knew she'd never forget it.

They stood there for what seemed an eternity,

but was really only a few minutes. Gabriel stepped away from her, grasped her by the shoulders, and pulled her around to stand in front of him. "I'm glad it was you," was all he said.

Mutely, Leeanne nodded. She understood what he meant. She wouldn't have wanted to share this with anyone but him either. She followed him inside.

The open house was winding down. Mr. and Mrs. McNab, with Mrs. Lourie in tow, caught up with Leeanne in the foyer. "We'll be giving Susan a ride home," her mother said airily. "Nathan says he wants to take you out for a bite to eat."

"Gee, Mom, thanks." Leeanne sputtered in surprise. Her shock increased as she saw her father whip out his checkbook and buttonhole Mrs. Drake by the reception desk.

Openmouthed, she gaped at him as he wrote out a check. "Your work here is wonderful," Gerald McNab said to the startled director. "I'm so glad my daughter has this chance to do something worthwhile. It's given her a whole new perspective on life."

Nathan stood beside her as they waved good-bye to their parents. "Ready?" he asked, turning and giving her a heart-stopping smile.

"Let me get my things," she murmured, suddenly scared at the prospect of what she was going to have to do.

"You're awfully quiet tonight," Nathan said. "You didn't say more than ten words at dinner."

"I guess I'm just tired." Leeanne smiled warily. He unlocked the car, climbed in, and reached across to unlock her door.

"Yeah," he said as he shoved the keys in the ignition. "You worked hard tonight. Uh, my mom really liked you. She liked your folks too."

"I liked her." Leeanne knew she couldn't delay much longer. She had to tell him the truth. She'd been lucky tonight, no one at Lavender House had given her away, but Gabriel was right, she was trapped in her own web and she wanted to be free of it. Gabriel. Thinking of him gave her courage. "Are you in any particular hurry?"

Nathan glanced at her in surprise. "No." He grinned slowly. "I don't have to be at work until ten tomorrow, so I can sleep in. Why? What did you have in mind?"

"I have to talk to you," she said.

"Talk," he teased. "Is that it?" His smile faded as he took in the seriousness of her expression.

"Nathan, it's important."

He nodded and turned his attention to getting them out of the coffee shop parking lot. "Where do you want to go?"

"There's a vacant lot right down the street from my house," she replied. "We can talk there."

They made small talk on the way to Leeanne's neighborhood and with every passing moment she felt her courage draining away.

"Over there." She pointed as he turned the car into the street where she lived.

He pulled up at the curb and killed the engine.

Then he turned to face her. "Is this going to be one of those I'm sorry, I don't want to see you again but we can still be friends kind of conversations?" He tried to keep his tone casual, but Leeanne could hear the fear in his voice.

Leeanne shook her head. Her palms were damp and her heart was hammering so loudly it was a wonder the car wasn't vibrating. "No, but after you hear what I've got to say, you may never want to speak to me again." She didn't really believe that, but she knew she had to be prepared for the worst.

"No way," he said. He leaned over and kissed her on the mouth. The kiss was sweet and gentle and she never wanted it to stop. But of course, it did. He finally pulled away. "All right, let's get this over with so we can get down to some serious kissing before I have to get you home." He flicked a quick glance at his luminous watch. "I promised your dad I'd have you in by midnight. It's almost eleven forty-five now, so talk fast."

She cleared her throat. "Well, I know you think you know me, but . . ."

"Think I know you?" he interrupted. "But I do know you and what I know, I like. We've spent a lot of time together in the last few weeks, you know."

"Yes," she countered. "But there are always things about someone that you, well, don't know . . ."

"I know everything that's important," he said earnestly. "You're honest and kind and jeez, Leeanne, you're about everything I've ever wanted in a girl."

Please God, she silently prayed, let him keep thinking that after tonight. "I'm glad you feel that way, I feel the same way about you. But how would you feel about me if you found out I wasn't so perfect, if you found out I wasn't so good, so much a saint? Would you still like me? Would you still want me to be your girlfriend?"

"Leeanne, what are you talking about?" he asked, his confusion evident from the puzzled tone of his voice. "I don't expect you to be perfect. And let's face it, you are altruistic. You give up most of your free time to volunteer at a hospice, for God's sake. Don't be so hard on yourself."

She felt like crying. "But that's just it. I'm not *giving* up my time."

"Huh?"

"Nathan, listen to me," she pleaded. "And try not to pass judgment until you hear me out, okay?"

"Okay," he agreed reluctantly.

Inwardly, she cringed at the suspicion she heard in his voice. "Right before school started, I . . . I." She hesitated as her courage deserted her.

"You what?" he prompted impatiently.

"I did something really stupid. Something I'm not proud of. I got arrested for shoplifting." She heard the hiss of his indrawn breath. Leeanne turned her head and stared straight ahead. It was hard enough telling him, she wasn't going to watch his face while she did it. "It was dumb and stupid and I did it because I wanted to impress my friends. Being arrested was the worst thing that ever happened to me. But the upshot of the whole thing was, I got sentenced to three hundred hours of community service. That's why I'm at Lavender House."

She closed her eyes. But he said nothing. The silence lengthened, she felt like a hot wire was being drawn around her heart and squeezing it shut. Finally, she couldn't stand it. "But I'm glad I was sent there. I met you and I'm doing something worthwhile and . . ."

"Cut the act." His words sliced through the air like cold steel. "You've been lying to me for weeks. Is that what I'm hearing?"

"I haven't been lying," she protested, "I just didn't want to risk telling you the truth. Not until we got to know each other better, not until you could get to know the real me."

He snorted derisively. "Oh, I think I got to know the real you all right. You're just another little rich girl slumming on the other side of the tracks. Only you weren't there because you wanted to be, you were there because you had no choice."

She looked at him and her heart sank. His face was a mask of contempt. His eyes burned with it, his mouth curved in a hard, flat line, and he'd backed himself against the door as though even being close to her might contaminate him.

"How can you say that?" she said. "What did I do that was so wrong? So I made a mistake. I got arrested for shoplifting. That doesn't make me an awful person. And I wasn't slumming. I'm glad I got sent to Lavender House."

"It's not the shoplifting," he snapped. "It's the fact that you've waited almost a month to tell me the truth! God, you must have had a great time," he sneered. "Every time I opened my mouth, you must have been laughing your head off. Why didn't you stop me? For crying out loud, you made a fool of me. You let me go on and on about how noble and dedicated you were."

"But . . ."

"And all the time you were there because you were doing time." He shook his head. "I can't believe I fell for it again. It's Gina all over again. Only with her, I was a way of getting back at her parents. What was it with you?"

"You were a guy I'm crazy about," she yelled. "That's what it was."

"Yeah, right," he said, sarcasm dripping from his voice like venom. "What did I represent to you, Leeanne. Penance? Go out with the poor boy from the wrong side of the tracks to make up for being stupid enough to get caught or was I just a little bit of entertainment on the side while you did your time?"

Her own temper flared. She'd been wrong to keep the truth from him, but she'd tried to correct that. He was overreacting way too much. "I went out with you because I liked you. The only thing you are to me is a person. A guy I really care about but who obviously still hasn't gotten over the bruising he took with his old girlfriend."

She unsnapped her seat belt and opened the door. Jumping out, she turned and looked at him. He was staring straight ahead. "I like you, Nathan, and I'm sorry I didn't tell you the truth sooner. But I wasn't using you and I wasn't laughing at you and I sure as hell wasn't doing penance with you."

He said nothing.

With a sick heart, Leeanne slammed the door and turned toward her house. She didn't hear his car start until she'd walked into her house.

Leeanne slept poorly. Alternately crying and cursing, she tossed and turned until the wee hours of the morning and then fell into a fitful sleep. Luckily, she didn't have to face her parents, they were taking part in an all-day bridge tournament at the country club. So she spent the day moping in her room and praying for the phone to ring. It didn't.

Monday morning it was hard to appear cheerful in front of her parents, but despite her breakup with Nathan, and she had no doubt they'd broken up, she didn't want to risk letting her parents suspect she was unhappy. There was still the chance they'd pull her out of the hospice. She forced herself to eat breakfast and talk eagerly about the open house.

"You know," her mother mused as she poured herself another cup of coffee, "I'm thinking I should cut back on my hours at work."

"That's a good idea," her father agreed. "We

could do with seeing you around here a little more often."

"Actually." She smiled sheepishly. "I was thinking that you could cut back on your hours too. We could do some volunteer work."

"Together?" Her father sounded surprised by the suggestion, but not altogether unhappy. "That's an idea. You know, I've been wanting to cut back lately. Work just hasn't given me all that much satisfaction recently. Maybe we should think about it."

"Well." Her mother gave Leeanne a warm smile and she forced herself to smile back even though it felt like her heart was cracked into itty-bitty little pieces. "Leeanne seems to have blossomed and after talking to Polly, and hearing how much joy she got out of giving her time . . ." She broke off, embarrassed.

Despite her misery, Leeanne was touched. "I know what you mean, Mom," she said, reaching over and patting her hand.

"I know it sounds corny," Eileen said, shrugging. "But last night I suddenly realized how much need there is in the world and well, how little we actually do to help."

"We give to charity," Gerald pointed out.

"True, but I think there's something about giving of yourself," her mother said thoughtfully. "I think it changes you."

Amen to that, Leeanne thought. She finished breakfast, kissed her Dad good-bye, and hurried out to catch a ride to school with her mom.

By the time she arrived at the hospice that afternoon, the warm fuzzies she'd gotten from her parents had completely evaporated and she was so far down in the dumps she didn't think she'd ever climb out.

Gabriel was waiting for her when she walked inside. "How did it go?"

"Lousy." She dumped her backpack behind the reception desk and stomped down the hall toward the broom closet. Yanking out the cleaning cart, she began stacking the supplies.

"That bad, huh?" Gabriel shifted uncomfortably. "Well, at least now you're not trapped in a lie. I mean, you don't have to worry about him finding out from someone else."

"Oh, no, I told him the truth, just like you said." She slammed a bottle of glass cleaner onto the top shelf. "Yeah, your advice was real good, Gabriel. Only guess what? Now I don't have a boyfriend."

Gabriel winced. "Hey, I'm sorry. But it's better to face the truth."

"Truth," she yelled. "What the hell good is truth? There's a good chance he'd never have found out."

"Don't bet on it, kid," he said. "He'd of found out. Sooner or later the truth has a way of coming out. Besides, if he really likes you, if he cares about you at all, he'll be back."

"He won't be back," she countered. She remembered the expression on Nathan's face, how he'd been so disgusted he couldn't even look her in the eyes. "I know it. I've lost him and it really hurts."

"Leeanne," Gabriel said, "the bottom line is, if he couldn't handle knowing the whole story, the whole truth about you, then it would never have worked out anyway. People who really care about each other can't have lies and secrets between them."

Her temper flared. Her life was a mess. The only guy she'd ever really, really liked thought she was a lying, conniving, heartless witch, and Gabriel had the nerve to give her lectures on truth. "You're real hung up on truth, aren't you, Gabe? Especially when you've got nothing to lose. Well let me tell you something, you're not the one who has to face the music."

"I've faced hard truths," he said. "And you know it."

That took the wind out of her sails. She closed her eyes and slumped against the door frame. "I'm sorry. I shouldn't be taking this out on you. It's not your fault."

He laughed harshly. "Cut the crap," he said, reaching over and pulling her around to face her. "It is my fault. You'd have never said a word to him if I hadn't goaded you into it. So stop being nice because I'm dying."

"All right," she snapped. "It is your fault and if you weren't so sick, I'd wring your neck."

He stared at her for a long moment and then threw back his head and laughed.

"This isn't funny, Gabe," she warned.

"I know." He stopped laughing and pulled her close. Wrapping his arms around her, he squeezed her tight. "I know, princess. It's not funny at all. You really like this guy and I screwed it up for you. But don't worry, things have a way of working out."

"No they don't," she said, her voice muffled against his chest. Not only had she lost Nathan, but she realized she wasn't going to have Gabriel much longer either. Tears sprang to her eyes and this time she didn't bother to fight them back.

"Nothing ever works out like we want," she sniffed. "And I don't believe in miracles anymore."

"That's where you're wrong, princess," he whispered, his lips hovering close to her ear. "Miracles happen every day. Sometimes you just don't see them."

Chapter
Eight

October 27

Dear Diary,

Life is the pits. Nathan hasn't called. I think
he hates me. I've given up. Maybe Gabriel was
right. If Nathan had really cared about me, he'd
have given me a chance. One part of me wants
to call him, but I'm afraid. He'd only hang up. I
guess I'm afraid to face him. I know, I know, I'm
probably being idiotic. After all, we only had a
few dates. But that doesn't matter. I still feel like
there's a great big gaping hole in my life. I saw
the guy every day and talked to him practically
every night on the phone. I miss him like hell.
And I'm still really mad at Gabriel too. I wish I
was a better person, but apparently, I'm not.
But if Gabe hadn't talked me into telling Nathan
the truth, I'd still have a boyfriend. The funny
thing is, my folks were so impressed by all the
nice things people said about me at the open

house that they've taken me off restriction. I can even use my car on weekends. Not that there's anyplace I want to go.

Leeanne closed her diary and glanced at the silent telephone. For the thousandth time, she reached for the receiver, caught herself, and drew back. What was the use? Nathan didn't want to talk to her. It had been two weeks since their breakup. The longest, most miserable weeks of her life. She couldn't eat, couldn't sleep, couldn't concentrate on her schoolwork. In short, she couldn't do anything but be depressed and pray for the darned phone to ring.

Suddenly it rang. She stared at it stupidly for a minute, then leapt for it, hoping it was Nathan. "Hello." There was a distinct click as the person on the other end hung up. "Rats," she muttered. "It was probably a wrong number."

Wearily Leeanne got off the bed, slipped on her shoes, and picked up her backpack. She had a test in French today, but she couldn't make herself care if she passed it or not.

School was a drag. The hours crawled past with the speed of a glacier. Because of her excellent study habits, two weeks of barely keeping it together hadn't made her grades drop by much. When the final bell rang, Leeanne handed in her French test and hurried out of the room. Jen met her in the hallway.

"Hi," she said with a wide smile. "Where have you been lately?"

"Same as usual," Leeanne replied. "Working at the hospice and studying. How about you?" The last thing she wanted was an inquisition from Jennifer. That was funny too, a couple of months ago and she'd have had the phone lines buzzing pouring out her troubles to her friend. But for some reason, she couldn't bring herself to confide in anyone about Nathan. Except Gabriel, of course. But only because it was all his damned fault and he deserved to hear her moan and groan.

Jen fell into step beside her as they meandered down the hall toward their lockers. "Oh, you know. Cheerleading practice and school. Oh, and going out with Todd, of course."

"That's nice." Frankly, Leeanne didn't much care if Jen was dating Freddy Krueger. She smiled faintly at the image. Come to think of it, maybe that would have been a good match. "Todd's a great guy."

"Are you still seeing Nathan Lourie?" Jen asked, her voice deceptively neutral.

Leeanne wasn't fooled for a minute. She knew what it meant when Jen used that tone. "Why do you ask?"

Jen shrugged. "Well, I just wondered, that's all. It's kinda funny, you see. I happened to mention Nathan to Ruby and it turns out, she knows him. They have some classes together at Landsdale JC."

Ruby was Jen's older sister. Leeanne knew she wasn't going to like what was coming next; Jen looked far too smug to be giving her anything but bad news.

"And Ruby said she saw Nathan at the movies on Saturday night with a cute blonde. I was kinda shocked. I mean, I thought you and Nathan had something going."

Leeanne felt like she'd been punched in the stomach, but she would die before she'd let it show. But she wasn't going to lie anymore. Lies hurt. No matter how hard it was on her pride, she wasn't going to pretend anymore.

"Nathan and I don't have a thing going," she said. "He's free to date whoever he likes. We're not seeing each other anymore."

"Oh." Jen feigned a look of surprise. "I see."

"Yeah." Leeanne smiled wearily. "I'll bet you do."

The bus ride to Lavender House was agony. Leeanne sat like a carved statue, afraid to blink her eyes in case she started crying. She jumped off the bus at her stop and didn't even look in the direction of the coffee shop. What good would it do? Nathan was already seeing someone else. The jerk.

She glanced up at the sky and frowned. Dark clouds were rolling in from the west. From the look of them, it would probably be pouring by the time her shift ended.

Leeanne rinsed the last of the cleanser out of the sink and wrung out her cloth.

"What the heck's taking you so long?" Gabriel

demanded. He was lying on his bed, watching her through the open bathroom door. "How long does it take to clean a sink?"

"Quit complaining," Leeanne snapped, her own mood was as bad as his appeared to be. "You want me to kill the germs, don't you?"

"Not particularly." He coughed. "Germs got a right to live too."

"All right," she said, coming into the room and tossing her cloth on the cleaning cart, "what's wrong? You've been nagging me since I got here. What's up?"

He leaned back against the pillows. "Nothing's up, I just wanted to talk."

"About what?" She peeled off her rubber gloves.

"About why you're so pissed at me."

"I'm not mad at you," she said. But she was and he knew it. She'd been furious at him for the last two weeks. Ever since the night she'd taken his "advice" and told Nathan the truth.

"Cut the act." Gabriel laughed. "You are mad. You're just keeping it all inside because you don't want to fight with someone who's dying."

Leeanne raised her chin and met his gaze. "Okay, so I'm a little annoyed with you. There, does saying it out loud make you feel better?"

"What would make me feel better is you being your old self," he snapped. "You've been sulking and moping around here for the last two weeks now and I'm sick of it."

"Well pardon me for having feelings," she cried,

snatching up the cleaning cart and stomping toward the door. "I'll just take my long face out of here so your highness isn't offended."

She would have slammed the door on the way out, but she didn't want to wake Jamie, who she knew was sleeping. Leeanne's anger carried her all the way down the hall to the upstairs cleaning cupboard. She tossed her supplies inside and closed the door. But by the time she was heading for the stairs, she couldn't stand it. Guilt, that ugly snake, coiled into her stomach and made her half sick. Gabriel meant too much to her, she couldn't leave it like this. Whirling around, she marched back into his room.

"Okay," she said bluntly, ignoring his triumphant grin, "let's talk."

"Couldn't handle it? Huh." He patted the bed and she flopped down.

"Oh, wipe that stupid smirk off your face. I'm here, aren't I? I just didn't want to leave with us still fighting." She noticed he winced in pain as the mattress shifted under her weight.

He sobered and reached for her hand. "I'm not smirking, Leeanne," he said softly, "I'm scared. I don't want to lose you. Not now."

A lump formed in her throat but she fought it back. She felt like a worm. "You're not going to lose me," she said gruffly, "you're just going to keep right on doing what you've always done. Annoying the heck out of me."

"Tell me why you've been so angry?" He stroked her hand.

She shrugged. "I don't know. I guess I just needed someone to blame."

"And I was a good target, right?"

"Right."

"But that's not all there is to it," he said. "Something else is bothering you. I want to know what it is."

"Don't be silly," she said. She'd die before she ever admitted to him what else had been bothering her about this whole episode. "Much as I hate to admit it, you gave me good advice. You were right. A relationship built on a lie isn't going to last. I guess I blamed you when it all blew up in my face. Nathan didn't exactly take it well. He was so . . . so . . ."

"Hurt?"

"Unreasonable," she corrected, dropping her gaze and staring at the bedspread. "But that's okay. If he'd really liked me he'd at least have made an effort to understand. I'm sorry I've taken it out on you. But like you said, I wanted someone to blame and you made a good target."

Gabriel reached over and lifted her chin, forcing her to meet his eyes. He stared at her intently, his eyes dark burning fire in his thin face. "But you started to wonder, didn't you? You started to wonder if maybe I didn't have an ulterior motive in giving you that advice?"

"Don't be silly." She tried to look away but he wouldn't let go of her chin. "What motive could you possibly have?"

He smiled sadly and Leeanne was suddenly desperate not to have him say anything else, not to have the words actually spoken out loud. "Please," she said, jerking her head away and scooting back on the bed. "Let's forget we ever had this conversation. Everything's okay now . . ."

"No it's not," he said. "You're not stupid. I think you know how I feel about you."

She froze. "We're friends."

"Friends?" He laughed harshly. "Yeah. We're friends all right, but even a half-wit could figure out I've fallen in love with you."

The words had been said. The words that she knew would break her heart and leave her lying in a thousand little pieces.

"But I swear to you, Leeanne," he continued softly, his gaze shifting to the window and the darkness beyond. "I didn't want you to tell Nathan the truth because I had any illusions that there could ever be anything between us. It's too late for that. I know the score. I'm going to be dead soon."

"Don't say that!"

"Why not? It's the truth. Believe me, much as I hated knowing you really liked the guy, I'm not dumb enough to think that if you busted up with him you'd come running to me. I care too much for you to do something that low. Besides, all in all, Nathan's pretty decent. I'd rather you were with someone like him than one of those arrogant little yuppies from your part of town."

She didn't know what to say. In the sudden silence she could hear the sounds of traffic mingling with the songs of the birds from outside the half-open window.

"Say something," he finally whispered. "Tell me that you believe me. Tell me that you know I'm not a selfish creep that tried to ruin your love life so I could have you all to myself."

"You're not a selfish creep, Gabe," she said.

"Thanks for that much," he sighed. "But I shouldn't have told you how I feel. You don't want to hear it."

"I don't know what to say," she murmured, but suddenly she did. Suddenly she knew why Gabriel could punch her buttons faster than anyone she'd ever met.

"Don't say anything," he said wearily. "There's no point."

But there was, Leeanne thought. Gabriel deserved to know the truth. She owed him that much.

"Yes there is," she said. She took a deep breath. "You were right. I did wonder if you had an ulterior motive. I did wonder if maybe you hadn't fallen for me yourself, because, well, the truth is, I think I'm a little in love with you too."

His jaw gaped open.

Leeanne would have laughed at the sight, if the subject had been anything except their feelings for one another. Feelings that confused her, tortured her, and kept her awake at night wondering what kind of a person she really was.

"But that's not possible . . ." she continued hesitantly, unsure of exactly what she meant or the best way to say it. "I mean, I really care for Nathan so how could I have these feelings for you?" Confused, she broke off.

Gabriel took a deep breath. "Who the hell knows? Our situation is hardly normal. By rights, we shouldn't have even met."

"Don't say that," she cried. "Don't ever say that. I don't understand my feelings for you. I've never felt like this before. You make me mad, sad, glad, guilty, everything. But I don't care. I know you're dying. And I know that one part of you thinks I'm a little rich girl playing around at being a saint, but please never, never be sorry you met me."

"I'm not sorry," he said softly. "I'm only sorry that it wasn't in another time or another place. I'm only sorry that I'm trapped in a body that's wearing out fast."

"But you don't know that," Leeanne said passionately. "Miracles do happen, you said so yourself."

He smiled sadly. "A miracle has happened. I met you, didn't I?"

"But what good has it done us," she said bitterly. "I don't know how I feel about you. I don't know how I feel about Nathan. Hell, I don't know anything anymore except that I'm being torn in two."

He reached over and touched her shoulder. "You'll never know how much good knowing you has done me," he said. "I'll never have the chance to take you to the movies or for a walk on the beach or to make love to you, but I thank God every single day that at least I got to have you in my life for a time. That is a miracle, Leeanne."

Leeanne burst into tears. "Oh, God," she moaned. "How can this be happening? How can I feel like this about you and still have feelings for Nathan? I don't understand."

"Hey," he said, reaching up and pulling her into his arms, "don't let it get to you. I don't understand it either. But what else is new? Besides, where is it written in stone that you can't care for two people at the same time? Where is it written that emotions come in nice neat little packages that you open whenever you want?"

"But it doesn't make sense," she said, swiping at her eyes. "I care for you, oh, God, Gabriel, I really do. But I still want him too. What does that make me?"

By the time her shift was over, it was pouring rain. Leeanne didn't much care. She knew her mom would come and get her if she called, but she wanted to take the bus. The confrontation with Gabriel may have cleared the air between them, but she felt like she'd been through the wringer.

Mrs. Drake loaned her an umbrella and Leeanne stepped out onto the front porch. Rain hammered against the umbrella as Leeanne ran across the street for the bus stop. Her feet got soaked as she jumped across a mini-river of water rushing in the gutter. She stood at the bus stop, staring through the blessed darkness down the street. Teary-eyed, she gazed at the wet reflections of the neon signs. The streams of blues and reds, golds and greens, seemed to move and blend into a rushing whirl of color as the rain and wind battered the black pavement. She stared hard at the road, feeling a sense of blessed peace ease her ragged nerves. A blast of frigid air sliced through her thin jacket, rain ricocheted off the seat of the bench and slapped against the back of her jeans, but she didn't move. She couldn't. The strange beauty of the neon in the rain held her rooted to the spot.

A car pulled up in front of her, causing her to blink.

"Hey." The driver leaned across the passenger side and rolled down the window. It was Nathan. "Get in," he yelled, "I'll give you a lift home."

She hesitated, not sure she could face him just now.

"Hurry up," he yelled, "you're getting soaked."

Leeanne quickly climbed inside. "Hi," she mumbled.

"Hi." He stared out the windshield, concentrating on the road.

Neither of them spoke as he pulled away from the curb and into the traffic. It was dark inside the car and she was glad about that.

"Uh, thanks for stopping and picking me up," she finally said.

"No problem," he said, still staring straight ahead. "I was going this way anyway."

They drove down Twin Oaks Boulevard in silence so strained that the air practically vibrated. Leeanne sat rigid, her eyes focused out the window.

"So." His voice sounded perfectly normal. "How's it going?"

"Fine. How about you?"

"No complaints," he said with a shrug.

She was too tired to make small talk, too drained to make any effort at all. Much as she liked Nathan, the next move was up to him. Leeanne didn't delude herself that his giving her a lift was anything except an act of kindness. She wasn't going to read anything into it. Her confrontation with Gabriel had set her straight about one thing, not facing how you really felt was stupid. Her eyes narrowed as she tried to put her finger on exactly what she did feel. Surprisingly enough, she was mad. Nathan had acted like a real jerk. And he hadn't called.

He pulled into the left-hand lane and turned onto MacGower Road. The traffic was a lot less heavy here. "Uh, Leeanne," Nathan began, "about what happened between us . . ."

"Let's not go into that," she interrupted politely. Angry or not, there was no reason to go over it again. Nathan probably thought his behavior was perfectly justified. If he couldn't see how crummy he'd behaved, he sure wouldn't believe it coming from her. "There really isn't any point. The past is over and done with."

"Yeah, well, I shoulda called you."

"It's all right."

"Are you going to be working at the hospice much longer?" Nathan asked. He gave her a quick glance and then turned his attention back to the rain-slicked road.

"Yeah, I've got a lot of hours to do yet," she said. "Besides, I like working there. Even after my CS is done, I'll see if they'll let me stay on."

"You know, there's no reason you can't come into the diner," he said. "I mean, you liked to come in and have a Coke before your shift started. Uh, Henry and some of the regulars have been asking where you are."

"Maybe I will," she said noncommittally. God, this was turning into the ride from hell. Nathan was obviously ill at ease and embarrassed. Whatever they'd once had between them was over. Dead and buried. All she wanted to do was get home, climb into bed, and lick her wounds. Why hadn't the lousy bus come instead of Nathan?

They didn't say anything else until Nathan had turned onto her street. But instead of stopping in front of her house, he drove on past and pulled up in the exact spot where they'd broken up. "Hey," she said, "what's the idea?"

He cut the engine and turned to look at her. "I want to talk to you."

She was suddenly too angry to keep it all inside. Who did he think he was? What did he want to do now, spend half an hour telling her what a lowlife conniving witch she was? Maybe what she'd done had been wrong, but she'd paid for it. He'd been a real jerk. "Why? You have some more interesting comments about my character? Well, why don't you save them. If it's all the same, I'll just pass. You made your opinion of me perfectly clear two weeks ago." She reached for the door handle.

"Leeanne, wait."

She stopped and turned to look at him. "For what? More insults?"

"I'm sorry," he finally said. "I know I acted like a real creep."

"True."

In the faint light from a streetlamp, she saw him grin. "You don't have to agree with me so fast," he said.

She said nothing. She was surprised by the depth of her own rage. He'd hurt her and been unfair to her and she was only now acknowledging that maybe the fault hadn't been all hers. But she wasn't going to sit here for another little heart-to-heart that was going to leave her cut and bleeding. She'd already done that number today and she didn't need a repeat performance. "What's this all about, Nathan? You don't have to give me the song and dance about being friends. I know what you think of me, so let's just leave it at that. Okay?"

"It's not okay! Unless you've become a mind reader you can't possibly know what I think of you." He started to get angry, caught himself, and took a deep breath. "Look, just hear me out, will you?"

She sighed. Maybe the fastest way to get this over with was to listen to what he had to say. Then she could go home and cry in peace. "All right."

The rain pounded hard against the roof of the car. Nathan shoved his hands in the pockets of his jacket and turned to stare out the windshield. "I really miss you, Leeanne," he said. "And I'd like to see you again?"

"As friends?" Leeanne asked warily.

He shook his head. "No. Friends isn't going to work, at least not yet. I'd like to try again. You know, going out and seeing how things work out. I haven't been able to stop thinking about you, to get you out of my mind."

"But what about all those things you said," she said. "If you're going to put me in the same category as your ex-girlfriend . . ."

"You're not at all like Gina," he interrupted. "I said those things when I was mad. I thought you'd been using me."

"Do you still think that?"

"No." He smiled slightly. "I think you really liked me and I know I really liked you."

"But you don't admire me much, do you?" She wanted everything out in the open. Her feelings were confused. The confrontation with Gabriel, the past two weeks of missing Nathan, she couldn't honestly say anymore how she felt about anything, least of all getting back together with Nathan. God, how she wished things were different. Simple. The way life used to be.

"Is it admiration you want?" he asked.

"No," she replied, determined to be equally blunt. "I never did. But I want honesty."

"Honesty, okay, I'll give you honesty. You're right, I don't feel the same way about you as before," he snapped. "I thought you were a saint and then I found out you're on probation."

"Then why do you want to keep seeing me?"

"Because I really, really like you, damn it. Because I can't get you out of my mind. I miss talking to you and I miss seeing you and a whole lot of other things." Nathan paused and took a deep breath. "Besides, you're the only girl I know who reads as much as I do. There, happy now?"

Leeanne laughed. "Yes. Because I've got a few things I want to say to you."

"Like what? Pardon me for pointing this out, but I've been absolutely honest with you from the first day we met."

"True," she agreed, "but you've also been judgmental, narrow-minded, and, well, self-righteous."

Nathan looked absolutely stunned.

"Self-righteous," he repeated softly, as though he'd never heard the term before. "Narrow-minded? Judgmental? You've got to be kidding."

"I'm not," she said. It was very important that she make him understand. "You were all those things. That night I told you the truth, you didn't cut me any slack at all. You jumped to conclusions about my character and my motivations, you passed judgment on me as a human being."

"I did not," he said. "Hell, I was shocked. How did you expect me to act?"

"I don't know," she replied. "But I expected a little more understanding than I got. It wasn't easy telling you the truth."

He opened his mouth, closed it, and stared down

at the steering wheel. "Jeez, Leeanne, I don't know what to say. I'll admit I acted like an idiot, but man, I was really freaked. You could have knocked me on my butt that night. It felt like I'd been slugged in the stomach. I thought you were so . . . so . . . good, I'd put you on this pedestal. Heck, I practically worshiped the ground you walked on. Here I was thinking you were a beautiful seventeen-year-old version of Mother Teresa and then all of a sudden you tell me you're not a saint at all, you're doing time. How would you have felt?"

"Lousy," she admitted. "But I'd like to think I'd at least have tried to understand. I'd like to think I'd have given you a chance. I can understand why you blew up at me that night. But it's been two weeks, Nathan, and you haven't even called. If you hadn't run into me tonight, would you have ever called?"

"I called you this morning, but I hung up when you answered the phone," he muttered. "And I didn't just happen to run into you tonight. I was watching for the bus today at work. I saw you get off. When it started to pour, I decided to make it look as if I'd just run into you and was doing my good deed for the day." He laughed. "Guess I'm not much of a saint either."

"Neither of us is a saint," she said. "We're just human beings."

"Are you trying to tell me that you don't want to try again?"

"No." She shook her head. "I'd like us to start over and see where it goes."

His shoulders relaxed and he smiled faintly. "Even though I'm a narrow-minded, judgmental jerk with no understanding or compassion."

"That's not true," she said. "You're not a jerk and you did have a good reason for getting upset. But the next time we have a fight, don't be so quick to judge me. And don't wait two weeks before you call me."

"It's been the longest two weeks of my life," he said. "I've missed you like crazy."

"Have you dated anyone else?" she asked, remembering what Jen had told her at school.

He put his hands on her shoulders and drew her closer. "My social life lately has consisted of *Star Trek* reruns and one hot date taking my cousin out for dinner and a movie."

"Your cousin?" She relaxed against him.

"Uh-huh." He leaned down and brushed his lips against hers. "What about you?" he murmured. "But I've gotta warn you. If you've fallen for someone else, I'll die of a broken heart."

Chapter
Nine

October 31

Dear Diary,

Boy, things have sure turned around for me. Nathan and I are back together and I think it'll be even better than before. I'm still confused about a lot of things, but I'm not letting it get me down. Mainly, I don't know what to do about Gabriel. My feelings for him are so tangled up I don't know whether I'm coming or going. I thought it might be hard seeing him, especially after our talk the other day, but it's been okay. He might have feelings for me, but you'd never know it by the way he acts. Teasing me is still his favorite sport. I'm a little worried though, he hasn't looked good the past couple of days and I've noticed he's spending an awful lot of time in bed.

Nathan and I are going to a Halloween party tonight.

Leeanne frowned as she looked at the diary entry she'd written over a week ago. The party had been fun, she enjoyed meeting Nathan's friends.

But she was still as confused as ever about Gabriel.

She turned to the next page, picked up her pen, wrote November 5th, stared at the words for a minute, and then closed her diary. She had no idea what to write. It seemed callous to scribble page after page about her and Nathan, especially as she was so worried about Gabriel. He wasn't doing well.

Leeanne glanced at the clock, decided to put off writing in her diary until she had something cheerful to say, and grabbed her purse. It was Sunday, and she'd been up early this morning baking cookies. No sense in letting the calories go to her hips. She might as well take a quick run over to the hospice and give them to Gabe.

Gabriel was lying on his bed. "What are you doing here on a Sunday?" he asked, his tone grumpy.

"Just thought I'd pop by and see how you were feeling," she said, pulling up a chair next to his bed and flopping into it. She placed the box of cookies she'd brought along on the bedside table.

He arched his eyebrows. "Well ain't I the lucky one?"

"How come you're in such a lousy mood?"

"How come you're so damned cheerful lately?"

Leeanne bit her lip. She hadn't told Gabe about

her and Nathan getting back together. She didn't know why, but somehow it seemed, well, tacky. "No reason," she said, "I'm just being my usual sunshiny self."

"Bull," he snorted and closed his eyes. "You don't have to try and spare me, Leeanne. You're back with Nathan."

She sighed. "Look, I wasn't trying to spare you."

"Good." He smiled faintly. "My ego's as strong as the next guy's, but thinking you were trying to shield my feelings because you felt sorry for me was driving me crazy."

"I wasn't doing that," Leeanne said hesitantly. But that was exactly what she'd done. "I just didn't want to talk about Nathan yet. Especially as we're sorta just feeling our way along."

"I'm glad for you," he said as he lay back against the pillow. He turned his head and nodded toward the box on the table. "Are there chocolate-chip cookies in that?"

There were dark circles under his eyes and pain lines bracketing the edge of his mouth. He'd been in bed now for two days and Leeanne was getting scared. She'd checked with the weekend duty nurse before coming upstairs, and she'd found that he hadn't been eating much lately.

"Is a pit bull mean? Of course those are cookies," Leeanne said lightly. "Do you want them now? I can run down to the kitchen and get you a glass of cold milk." Please God, she prayed silently, let him eat something, even if it is just sweets.

"Nah, I'll have them later." He winced as he

shifted position, trying to get more comfortable. "I'm a little tired now."

"But they're your favorite," she protested and then clamped her mouth shut. Gabe would know what she was trying to do if she kept on nagging him. "But later is fine, you can tell me how wonderful they were tomorrow."

"They'll be great, princess," he said, a smile curving his lips. "Why don't you read to me?"

"Sure." She got up and headed toward the bookcase. "What do you want me to read?"

"What do you think? Asimov, of course."

"Which one? You've got practically everything the man wrote here."

He laughed softly. "No way. He wrote hundreds of books. I've only got a few dozen. Read me *Foundation*."

Leeanne's hands trembled as she pulled out the old paperback. He was sick. Really sick. And she was scared to death.

Sitting back down, she glanced at Gabe and saw that his eyes were closed. But she knew he wasn't sleeping. Opening the book, she started to read.

For half an hour, she read to him. She would have been quite happy to read to him for the rest of the day, but Mrs. Drake came in and said that Gabriel was sound asleep. Leeanne didn't care if he was asleep or not. She didn't want to leave. But the director didn't give her much choice, she motioned her out of the room.

"What are you doing here on a Sunday?" Mrs. Drake asked when they were outside the door.

"I just wanted to see how Gabe was doing."

Mrs. Drake gazed at her, her face a mixture of exasperation and sympathy. Finally, she smiled. "I know. You two are pretty close, aren't you?"

"Yeah, we've become good friends."

"Come on downstairs," Mrs. Drake commanded. "Let's go have a cup of coffee. I need to talk to you."

In the kitchen they helped themselves. When they were seated at the kitchen table, Leeanne braced herself for the worst. Was the director going to order her to stay away now that Gabriel was so ill?

Mrs. Drake picked up her mug, took a sip, and gave Leeanne a warm smile. "You're really something, you know that? I think I owe you an apology."

Stunned, Leeanne gaped at her. "An apology," she sputtered. "But why? You haven't done anything." Not yet anyway. Maybe she was apologizing because she was getting ready to let the ax fall on visits to Gabe.

"I'm apologizing for the way I talked to you the day you first came here. You're not a thief. You're just one heck of a nice kid who got caught pulling a prank that probably half the teenagers in America do." She sighed. "I'm really sorry, Leeanne. You've been one of the best volunteers we've ever had."

"Thank you," Leeanne said. She felt her cheeks turn pink. "But the truth is, I'm kinda glad I got arrested. If I hadn't, I'd never have come here and well . . . I don't even like to think about that. I love working here, it's kinda changed my life." She paused in confusion. Had she really said something that lame? She had. Even worse, it was the truth. This place had changed her life. No, she thought quickly, not this place. *These people* had changed her life.

"It changes everyone," Mrs. Drake said. "Working with our patients gives you tired feet, tired backs, sore hands, a lot of laughs, and"—she paused and looked Leeanne directly in the eye—"a lot of heartache. Lavender House is a place of joy and of sorrow, of pain and of compassion."

Leeanne stared at her for a long moment. Then she asked the question she wasn't sure she wanted answered. "Mrs. Drake, exactly how sick is Gabriel right now? I mean, he's just a little tired, right? He will bounce back."

The director looked down at her coffee cup and then back up at Leeanne. "No," she replied gently. "I'm afraid he won't. Not this time. Gabriel is dying."

"Leeanne. Earth to Leeanne." Nathan snapped his fingers under her nose.

"Hey." She batted his hands away. "Don't do that. I'm listening."

"Then how come you haven't spoken in five minutes," he complained as he reached for his glass of cola. "I've asked you the same question three times." At her blank stare he sighed dramatically. "I repeat. How was Gabe doing today?"

"How did you know I saw him?" she asked.

"Your mom told me." He took a sip. "Why? Was it a secret?"

Leeanne shook her head. Nathan had come over to tutor her in physics. She had a midterm scheduled for the next morning. But he might as well have been tutoring a wall, she sure as heck hadn't heard a word he'd said. Her concentration was shot. In her mind, she kept hearing Mrs. Drake say those awful words. "Gabriel is dying." The phrase kept repeating itself over and over, like a broken record.

"Gabe's not doing too well," she muttered, looking down at the open physics text on the kitchen table.

"I'm sorry," Nathan said softly. He reached over and covered her hand with his. "You're really upset, aren't you?"

She couldn't find her voice to answer him. A great big lump had tightened her throat so she just nodded her head. Nathan didn't say anything, he just sat beside her, his warm hand covering hers, and let her take long, deep breaths.

Finally, when she thought she could talk without breaking down and sobbing like a baby, she said, "I didn't think it would hit me like this. Sorry for being such a wimp."

"Don't apologize, babe." He put his arm around her shoulder. "You're hurting. I can see that. Exactly how bad is he?"

She opened her mouth, but she couldn't get the words to come. Saying it out loud would make it real. So she shrugged instead and hoped he'd understand.

"All right, I think I get the picture," he said. "But when you do want to talk about it, let me know."

"Leeanne, Nathan," her mother's voice came from the kitchen door. "That doesn't look like studying."

Leeanne groaned softly. Nathan quickly pulled away from her and grinned sheepishly at Mrs. McNab. "Uh, it's not what it seems," he sputtered.

"Sure," she replied, laughing. "And I just won the lottery." Her laughter died as she noticed her daughter's haunted expression. She looked from Leeanne to Nathan, a concerned frown on her face. "Is everything all right?"

Leeanne still couldn't get her voice to work.

"Gabriel Mendoza is in a bad way," Nathan explained hastily. "Leeanne's pretty upset."

"Oh, honey," her mother said.

The telephone rang. In the quiet kitchen, the sound was frightening. Ominous.

Mr. McNab stuck his head through the door. "Leeanne," he called. "Telephone. It's Mrs. Drake from the hospice. She says it's urgent."

"Do you want me to take it?" Nathan asked.

Leeanne shook her head. Her legs felt like lead and time seemed to slow to a crawl as she walked across the kitchen to the extension. She picked up the receiver and listened. She was aware of Mrs. Drake's voice on the other end of the line. She heard the sound of Nathan's breathing and saw the

worried, warning look her mother threw her father.
Then she heard herself say, "All right, I'll be right
there."

Nathan stood up. He didn't have to ask what was
wrong. He knew. "I'll drive you."

"Leeanne," her father said, "I don't think you
ought to be going anywhere. This is a school night
and you have a midterm tomorrow."

She froze.

"Gerald." Her mother stood up. "Forget the
midterm. Leeanne's friend needs her. That's much
more important."

"But, Eileen," he argued, giving his wife a puzzled frown, "if she flunks physics her chances at
getting accepted at a decent college go right down
the drain. Besides, I don't really think a bedside
vigil is appropriate for a girl her age."

"If she lets Gabriel die without saying good-bye
she'll regret it the rest of her life," her mother said
sharply. "And as for flunking physics, well, I'd say
comforting a friend who's going to meet his maker
is a damned sight more important than getting into
a decent college. She can go to Landsdale JC for
all I care."

Surprised, Leeanne stared at her mom.

"Your working at Lavender House hasn't just
changed you," her mother said. "It's changed us
all." She kissed Leeanne on the cheek. "Go to Gabriel. Stay with him as long as he needs you. Call
me when you're ready to come home. I'll come get
you."

*   *   *

It was nine-thirty by the time she got to Lavender House. Nathan dropped her off in front, kissed her forehead, and told her to call him when she could.

Mrs. Drake and the duty nurse were standing on the other side of Gabe's bed when she opened the door and stepped inside his room. "He's been asking for you," Mrs. Drake said.

"Thank you for calling me," Leeanne replied. She tiptoed closer to the bed.

"I promised, didn't I?" Mrs. Drake smiled sadly. "He's resting now, but he keeps drifting in and out of sleep." She and the nurse left, leaving Leeanne alone with him.

She sat down next to his bed and began to silently pray. His breathing was soft and shallow, his skin pale against the darkness of his hair. She reached out and touched his hand, wanting to assure herself that life still pulsed in his flesh. The moment her fingers brushed his, he opened his eyes. "What took you so long?" he said, his voice so low she could barely hear him.

"Sorry." She tried to smile. "Next time I'll be faster."

His lips curved in the ghost of a grin. "There won't be a next time, princess."

"Don't be silly," she whispered, fighting back tears. "You're just tired, that's all. Come tomorrow, you'll be fine."

But she knew that wasn't true. So did Gabriel.

He closed his eyes for a long moment and she thought he'd drifted back to sleep. Then his fingers curled around hers. "Come closer," he said. "I want to talk."

"No," she cried, panicking. "You've got to save your strength. You've got to fight, Gabe. Hang on. You can beat this thing."

"Shhh." He sighed. "I can't. I don't want to. Damn it," he croaked, his voice a harsh whisper, "lean closer, I've got things to say and I don't have much time."

Tears pouring down her cheeks, she did as he instructed. "Don't, Gabe," she pleaded, "don't do this. I can't stand it if you . . ."

"I love you, princess," he interrupted.

"Oh, God, I love you too," she sobbed.

"I want you to do something for me."

"Anything," she said, swiping at her falling tears. "I'll do anything you want."

"That's a first." He made a sound that could have been a laugh, but he was so weak it came out like a cough.

"Don't try to talk, Gabe," she cried, trying to pull away so she could ring the call button for the nurse. "I'll call Mrs. Drake, we'll get you to the hospital . . ."

"No," he croaked. "No hospital, no doctors, and no damned machines. If you love me, if you really care for me, you'll let me die with dignity. All I want now is you . . . all I want is to tell you . . ."

Defeated, she slumped against the side of the bed, her face inches from his against the pillow. "All right," she whispered. "I'm here and I'll stay till the end. But you don't have to tell me anything. The effort is too much for you."

"Jeez," he snorted faintly, "give it a rest, Leeanne. I'm not dead yet. My vocal cords still work." With great effort, he raised his hand and laid it on her head, his fingers tangling in her hair. "I want to touch you one last time."

Leeanne cried softly, her tears running down her face and into the side of his neck.

"Can you hear me?" he whispered.

"Yes."

"Two things." His voice was fading. "I want to know something. I want to know that if we'd met in another time and another place, could you have loved me?"

"I do love you," she cried passionately. "You're the best friend I've ever had . . ."

"Could you have loved me as a man?" he asked.

Leeanne didn't even have to think about it. "Oh, yes, Gabriel. One part of me has always loved you that way."

"Thanks for that much," he said slowly.

She leaned closer. He was slipping away from her, his voice fading. "What else do you want to tell me?"

"Remember me."

"Of course I'll remember you," she promised.

"Remember me when the night birds sing." His voice was so soft she could barely make out the words. "Listen for them . . . know that I'll be with you always . . . every time you hear them sing . . ."

"Gabriel," she prompted. Panicked, she sat up and touched his face. He didn't move, his eyes were closed. Leeanne leaned across him and frantically jabbed the call button for the nurse.

"Gabriel," she repeated.

The nurse and Mrs. Drake hurried inside, but Leeanne paid them no attention. She was still saying Gabriel's name when Mrs. Drake pulled her away from the bed and out of the duty nurse's way.

"He's in a coma," the nurse said.

"For God's sake," Leeanne cried. "Wake him up. Call the paramedics." She started back toward the bed, but Mrs. Drake grabbed her arm.

"Leeanne," the director said firmly, "he's dying. We can't wake him up."

"We can try!"

Mrs. Drake grabbed her by the shoulders and gave her a gentle shake. "Listen to me. We're going to respect Gabriel's wishes. There's not going to be any paramedics, any hospitals, or any heroic gestures here. That's what he wanted. To die with dignity with someone he loved. That person is you, Leeanne. He wanted you here with him, so for goodness' sake get ahold of yourself."

"No," she wailed, furious that they were just giving up and letting him go. "Can't we at least try to do something . . ."

"There's nothing anyone can do," Mrs. Drake said harshly. "It's in the hands of God now and if you can't handle it you'll have to leave."

"Leave?" The very idea was unthinkable. Leeanne took a deep breath and closed her eyes for a moment. "No, I can't go. I've got to be with him, no matter how painful it is."

"It may be a while before . . ."

"That doesn't matter," Leeanne said softly. "I'll stay as long as it takes. But I won't let him die alone."

Leeanne pulled away and went back to Gabriel's bedside. She slipped into the chair and reached for his hand. Her mind was a complete blank. She would have prayed, but she couldn't get the words to come.

The hours passed slowly. Leeanne didn't take her gaze off Gabriel. Mrs. Drake and the nurse came in several times to check him. They brought her coffee, left it on the bedside table, but she didn't drink it. She didn't need caffeine to help her stay awake tonight.

Eleven o'clock passed and he still breathed. Leeanne decided that if he lived past midnight, he'd be okay. The only time she took her eyes off him was to glance at her watch.

Midnight came. He lived.

Leeanne leaned close to him and began to talk. On TV she'd seen the power of love, the power of words pull someone out of a coma. "Gabe," she whispered. "Don't leave me. I love you. I can't stand to think of this world without you. You're the best friend I ever had. You made me see things, you made me think, you made me feel . . ."

She thought she saw a faint smile curve his lips, but she wasn't sure.

One o'clock and still he breathed.

Two o'clock. His breathing became so shallow she could barely see his chest move.

It was almost three o'clock before he went. Just before that last moment, the moment when she knew he was gone forever, she felt his fingers grip her hand. "Kiss me," she thought she heard him whisper.

"Gabriel?" but when she looked at his face, his eyes were still closed. She leaned over and gently brushed her mouth against his. The faint grip on her fingers relaxed.

Gabriel was gone.

Leeanne had no idea how long she sat there, too numb to even reach over and press the call button for Mrs. Drake. It could have been minutes, it could have been hours. Finally, they came in, took one look at her face, and knew he'd died.

"Leeanne." Mrs. Drake reached down and gently unclasped Leeanne's fingers from his. "Come on, he's gone now. There's nothing for you here. Let's go down to the kitchen."

"But I promised I'd stay with him," she babbled.

"He's gone," the director insisted, pulling Leeanne to her feet and tugging her toward the door. "The nurse has things she's got to do. Legal and medical things. And I need to talk to you."

Leeanne let herself be hustled out of the room, but just before the door closed, she looked back and saw the nurse pull the sheet over Gabe's face.

In the kitchen, Mrs. Drake made them cocoa.

She put a mug in front of Leeanne and sat down opposite her. "Leeanne, how do you feel?"

"Numb," she replied. "I don't feel anything." If she let herself feel, the pain would kill her.

"That'll probably last for a little while," Mrs. Drake said sympathetically.

Leeanne nodded. There were questions she knew she should ask. Lots of questions. It was important. "The funeral," she said, "there has to be a funeral. He didn't have any money, but I've got some in my college fund . . ."

"It's all taken care of," Mrs. Drake interrupted. "Don't worry about it. Gabriel knew he was dying. He was legally an adult and he took care of everything."

"Oh, God," she moaned, "I can't believe this."

"I know." The director took another sip of cocoa. "Gabriel wanted me to be the one to tell you."

"Tell me what?" Leeanne asked dully. What more was there left to know? He was gone. She'd never see him again. And there was a great big hole somewhere inside her now that could never be filled again.

"You're his heir," Mrs. Drake said. She smiled at the stunned expression on Leeanne's face. "He didn't have much. But what he did have, he left to you."

The next few days were a foggy haze to Leeanne. Accompanied by her parents and Nathan, she sat through the funeral service and tried to relate the words of the minister to Gabriel Mendoza. But it sounded like he was talking about someone else. For one crazy moment, Leeanne wondered if they'd come to the right church. But Mrs. Drake and Mrs. Thomas and Polly were sitting in the pew right in front of her, and the pew behind her was filled with Gabe's friends from his old neighborhood. It was the right funeral. He was gone. Dead. She'd never see him again.

At the burial service, she stood by his casket and told herself he was at peace, but the words were cold comfort. He might be at peace, but those were only words. He was dead. Gone.

And she was really angry.

She forced herself to go back to school and tried hard to actually pay attention in class. Before long, she'd learned that if she sealed her emotions into a tight little corner of her heart, she could actually get through the day.

Her parents were concerned about her, she could see it in their eyes, so she tried hard to pretend that everything was just fine.

But she didn't fool them.

A couple of days after Gabe's funeral, Leeanne was sitting at her bedroom window staring at the sky when she saw Nathan pull into the driveway. Puzzled, because he hadn't called or anything, she went down to meet him.

"What are you doing here?" she asked. "I thought you had to work today."

"The electricity blew and nothing, but nothing works." Nathan grinned. "So Henry had to shut for the day."

"Well, good," she said, "so you get the day off."

"Yeah." He leaned back against the door of the car. "Mrs. Drake called me."

"She called you? Why? She told me I didn't need to come back to work until next week."

"It wasn't about your working," Nathan said quickly. "And she called me because she . . . uh . . . didn't want to upset you."

"What did she want?" Leeanne asked.

"She wanted me to come by and get Gabriel's things," he said softly.

"What things?"

"Books, paintings. You know, his personal stuff." Nathan stepped closer and pulled her against him. "It belongs to you now, Leeanne. Mrs. Drake was afraid you'd get upset if she asked you, but I thought you had a right to do it. You really cared about him. Taking care of the stuff that meant a lot to him is sorta the last thing you can ever do for him. Do you think you can handle it?"

She wasn't sure. "I don't know . . ."

"If you'd rather I go do it," he asked.

"No," she made up her mind. Nathan was right. This was the last thing she'd ever get to do for Gabriel. She wanted to do it. She wanted to pack up his books and fold his clothes and wrap his paintings. "I'll do it."

Nathan held her at arm's length and studied her face. "You really loved him, didn't you?"

"Yes," she admitted. She stared at Nathan, wondering if he had any idea of *how* she'd loved Gabe. She wasn't sure herself. Had it only been the love of one friend to another? Or had it been more? She didn't know anymore. "He was a very special person. He shouldn't have died."

"You're a very special person," Nathan said gently, pulling her close and burying his face in her hair. "And I'm glad you were there for him. I just hope you'll always be there for me too."

"I will," she promised. But she wasn't sure that was a promise she could keep. Life, she'd discovered, could play hell with the best of intentions. Who knew what would happen? Who knew how they'd feel about each other a year from now. There were no guarantees. The universe wasn't fair.

Chapter

Ten

January 7th

Dear Diary,

I haven't written in a long time—there hasn't been a lot I'd like to say. People say life goes on. But sometimes I think those are just words. I got through Thanksgiving and Christmas okay, but it was hard. I kept thinking that Gabe sure would have loved my mom's turkey and dressing or that maybe I'd get him a boxed set of Asimov for a present. Then I'd remember that he was dead.

I'm still working at the hospice. They made me take a few weeks off after Gabe died. But even with having to make up those hours, my community service will be finished soon. I'm not sure whether or not I'll keep on volunteering. Oh, heck, I might as well tell the truth, the place holds some pretty hard memories for me. I can't even stand to go into Gabe's room. It's occupied by a nice lady right now and I suspect she thinks I'm avoiding her. It's not her, it's all those memories. All those times we sat on his bed and argued about books and who wrote classic SF and who didn't.

Nathan and I are still together, but I don't know how long that's going to last. We had a huge argument last night, and it was all my fault. I don't know what's wrong with me. I'm just so mad at the whole world.

Leeanne sighed and put down her pen. What was the point? Spilling her guts didn't help. The past few months had been awful. She couldn't stop thinking about Gabe. She thought she'd hid it pretty well. Her grades were good and her parents, except for an occasional funny look from her mom, thought she'd adjusted just fine to losing her best friend. She'd gotten real good at putting on an act. But it still hurt like hell.

She turned around and stared at the opposite side of her room. Wrapped in heavy brown paper and neatly stacked against the wall were Gabriel's three paintings, half a dozen boxes of books, and two plastic bags of his clothes and personal things. She hadn't even gone through them. She couldn't. It was too painful. One of these days she'd take care of doing something with them, but not now. Not yet.

"Leeanne," her mom yelled from downstairs. "Nathan's here and we're leaving. We should be back by ten."

"Okay, Mom," she called. "Have a good time."

A few minutes later she heard Nathan's footsteps on the stairs. "Hi," he said.

She turned around in her chair and stared at him. "I'm surprised you came."

He shrugged and plopped down on the foot of her bed. "We had a date, remember?"

"We also had a fight, remember?"

Nathan leaned forward, his elbows propped on his knees. "Yeah, I remember it real well. But so what? Lots of couples have fights."

"Oh," she said sarcastically, "so you still consider us a couple."

He sighed and rolled his eyes. "Yeah. Why, do you want out?"

Did she? She didn't know. She only knew that since losing Gabriel her whole world had seemed out of whack. She felt like an actor who'd accidentally wandered into the wrong play. "No," she said softly. "I don't want to lose you."

"Then why don't we try and get at what's really going on here."

Leeanne's temper flared. "The only thing going on was you acting like a jerk."

"I'll admit I wasn't in the best of moods last night," he said, regarding her speculatively. "But you deliberately set out to start an argument. And that's not the first time. Why? If you don't want to go with me anymore, all you have to do is say the word."

"You're not a psychologist yet, Nathan," she said. "So stop pretending you see some kind of psychological pattern in my behavior. And you know how I feel about you."

"Do I?" He leaned back on the bed. "Lately it seems like everything I say, do, or think irritates the hell out of you. All I did last night was suggest that maybe we *shouldn't* spend so much time alone. And you'd have thought I was suggesting you slit your throat."

"Well how would you like it if I'd told you that I thought we ought to go out with other people," she snapped.

"That wasn't what I suggested, Leeanne," he said, still staring at her with that same look on his face. "I suggested we go out as a couple with some friends of mine."

She'd been wrong and she knew it, so she said nothing. But God, how could she make him understand? How could she make anyone understand when she didn't understand herself. It was like there was something inside her, something hateful and twisted that made her say things and do things she knew were stupid. But she couldn't help herself.

"But it wasn't what I said that pissed you off," he continued calmly. "You were already mad when I picked you up."

"That's not true."

"Oh, you're good," he said, "I'll give you that. You've got everyone fooled. Mrs. Drake, your teachers, your parents, but the bottom line is, it's all an act."

"An act!" she said. "I don't know what you're

talking about and neither do you. So you can cut the amateur shrink number."

"You're angry, Leeanne," he replied calmly. "Really angry and you're taking it out on me. You've been taking it out on me since Gabe died."

She leapt to her feet. "Bull. Gabe's death doesn't have anything to do with us."

Nathan reached over, grabbed her arm, and tugged her down on the bed beside him. "Yes it does," he said firmly. "And the only reason I've let you get away with it was because I understood. I felt the same way when my dad died. I was mad as hell and I wanted someone to lash out at so I took it out on my mom."

"I'm not taking anything out on you," she yelled.

He ignored that. "But I'm getting really sick of it. You're nowhere near coming to terms with losing Gabe, and I'm tired of you taking it out on me."

"So what are you saying?"

He stood up. "I'm saying, give me a call when you figure out who you're really pissed at. Then *maybe* we can work things out." He turned and stalked out of her room.

Too stunned to react, Leeanne stared at the empty doorway for a moment. She heard the front door slam. Without thinking, she ran after him.

"Nathan, wait," she called as she flew down the stairs and out the front door toward the driveway. "Please wait. I'm sorry."

But the car had already backed out of the drive and he didn't hear her.

* * *

Leeanne spent most of the night alternating between tears and anger. At school, she concentrated grimly on getting through the day. By the time the last bell rang, she'd made up her mind. She was going to have to take the first step. She'd already lost too much, she didn't want to lose Nathan as well.

The bus ride seemed to take forever, but eventually she found herself standing outside the diner. Taking a deep breath, she pushed open the door and stepped inside.

Nathan was standing at the counter refilling coffee cups for some of the regulars. He glanced up and saw her coming toward him.

"Henry," he yelled toward the back, "I'm taking a break." He held up the coffeepot and said to Leeanne, "Want some?"

She nodded and continued walking toward the back of the restaurant. At least Nathan was still willing to talk to her. Sliding into the booth, she took another deep breath as she waited for him.

He put the cups down and sat down opposite her. "Okay," he said, "I'm assuming you came for one of two reasons. You're either going to tell me to go to hell, or you're going to start being honest with me. Which is it?"

"You sure get right to the point, don't you?" She picked up the heavy cup and took a sip, not because she wanted any coffee, but because it would delay having to face him.

"Which is it?" he repeated.

"I'm going to start being honest," she said, looking down at the tabletop. "I don't want us to break up."

He sighed in relief. "Good. You mean a lot to me, Leeanne. I didn't want to blow this."

"What did you mean yesterday?" She finally found the courage to look at him. "About me not coming to terms with Gabe's death?"

"Exactly that," he said, giving her a gentle smile. "There's still one part of you that's really angry about it and you haven't allowed yourself to acknowledge those feelings. It's got you tied up in knots."

"That's how I've felt," she admitted. "Like I just wanted to kick something or someone only there wasn't anyone to kick. I mean, there's no point in being so angry. Who am I going to get mad at? God? The doctors? Fate? The universe? Fat lot of good that would do me."

"The point is, who are you mad at?" he probed softly. "Have you figured that out yet?"

She looked down again. Tears sprang to her eyes and her heart slammed against her chest. She didn't want to admit it. She didn't want to say the words out loud but if she didn't, she was going to drown in her own poison.

"Yeah," she whispered. "I think so. I'm mad at him."

"Who?" Nathan continued relentlessly. "Who are you angry with? Say it, Leeanne. Get it out of your system so you can get on with your life."

She clenched her hands into fists. A red mist of

rage tore through her at the speed of light and hot tears rolled down her cheeks. "Gabriel, oh, God, I'm so mad at him I could scream. How could he do it? How could he die like that? He didn't even try." She covered her face with her hands and cried softly.

Nathan said nothing. But after a few minutes, she felt his hand gently stroke her head. She let the tears pour out of her and as they fell, she felt some of the pain and anger and misery drain away as well.

"Let's go in the back," Nathan said softly. He got up and hustled her into a small pantry just inside the kitchen door. Pulling her close, he wrapped his arms around her and let her sob against his chest. "Get it out, get it all out."

"How can I feel this way?" she asked. "Gabe didn't want to die."

"Of course he didn't," Nathan said. "No one his age wants to go. But it's natural that you'd be angry at him. I felt the same way when my father died. I was so angry at him for leaving us . . . Hell, Leeanne, it doesn't make sense. But that doesn't mean the feelings aren't real. Who said human beings were rational."

She pulled away and smiled up at him. "I'm certainly not. All this time I've been so mad at Gabe that I could spit, even though I knew that feeling like this was stupid. Gabe was the last person who wanted to die. He loved life."

Nathan studied her for a moment. "Feel better?"

Oddly enough, she did. For the first time in weeks, she didn't have a knot of pain rattling hard inside her chest. "Yeah, I guess I do."

Leeanne wasn't sure if it was her talk with Nathan or simply fate that made her pick up the newspaper that afternoon. Mrs. Thomas, of course, said it was the hand of God.

She was doing dinner trays in the kitchen. As soon as she tucked the last set of silver into a napkin, she poured herself a cup of coffee and picked up the newspaper. There were still ten minutes before she had to take the trays up, and she thought she'd kill a little time.

Flicking through the pages, the words "art contest" leapt out at her. Leeanne's heartbeat quickened as she quickly scanned the short article.

"Mrs. Thomas," she said, her voice rising in excitement. "Look at this. There's going to be an art show. It's sponsored by the Department of Recreation. It's a contest. It's part of the Landsdale Centennial Celebration."

"Isn't that nice," the cook said, glancing over Leeanne's shoulder. "Paintings, drawings, and pottery . . . first prize is a thousand dollars," she read aloud. Nodding her head, she said to Leeanne, "You should enter one of Gabe's paintings."

"That's exactly what I was thinking."

As soon as she got home that night, Leeanne tore up to her room. Grabbing the three paintings, she immediately ripped off the heavy brown wrapping paper on the first one. It was the one he'd painted right before he'd died. He'd called it "Blackbird and City Scene."

The second one was another view. This one of a park right off Twin Oaks Boulevard. It was gorgeous. You could almost smell the scent of grass and touch the leaves on the trees. But it was the third one that almost sent Leeanne into shock.

She tore the last of the wrapping off and gasped. It was a portrait of her. Gabe must have painted it from memory. There was nothing showy or seductive or sophisticated about this painting. She was wearing jeans and a sweater, standing in the open bathroom door of Gabe's room, her arms folded across her chest and a cheeky grin on her face. Her box of cleaning supplies was at her feet.

Leeanne shook her head and began to laugh. Only Gabe would paint a woman right after she'd just scrubbed a bathroom. But it was the most beautiful painting Leeanne had ever seen.

It took her forever to decide which painting to enter in the art show. Finally, after consulting with Nathan, Mrs. Thomas, Polly, and her parents, she decided to enter the one he'd painted before he died. The one of the bird and the street scene in front of Lavender House. Leeanne wasn't interested in the prize money, but she was determined that the world would get to see Gabriel's talent.

It was the last thing she'd ever be able to do for him.

The day of the art show, Nathan picked her up and they drove to the square in front of the Landsdale City Hall. Everyone was there. Polly, Mrs.

Drake, Mrs. Thomas, her parents, even Henry and a couple of the regulars from the diner showed up.

Bright sunshine filled the festive square. There were craft booths, food booths, fortune-tellers, and speeches from the city fathers.

At four o'clock, they made their way to the art show. The winners of the contest weren't going to be announced till four-thirty, but Leeanne wanted to see the other entries. Holding Nathan's hand, they wandered up and down the rows. There were portraits, oil paintings, watercolors, sculptures, and just about everything else under the sun. But there was nothing that came close to Gabe's painting. At least that was Leeanne's opinion.

At four-thirty, they pushed their way through the crowd that had gathered on the steps of the city hall. Butterflies erupted in Leeanne's stomach as an elegant, dark-haired woman made her way to the microphone.

"Good afternoon, ladies and gentlemen. I'm Elizabeth Denholm, the director of the Art Department at Landsdale Junior College."

"I hope we don't have to listen to a bunch of speeches," Nathan whispered in Leeanne's ear.

"Shhh . . . I don't want to miss anything," Leeanne shot back.

"Now, without further ado," the director continued. "We'll get right to the winners."

"Oh, God," Leeanne moaned. "I'll die if he doesn't win."

"Whether he wins or not isn't the point," Nathan said. "People got to see his work. You saw how many people are here today. There was a whole bunch standing in front of his painting. I heard one man say he'd like to buy it."

"Our third place winner is Cathy Selkirk for her painting of the ocean at sunrise." There was a round of applause as the artist stepped forward and received her ribbon and prize money.

"In second place," the director continued brightly, "is Anthony Magill for his sculpture titled 'World Without End.'"

They waited while the long-haired and rather slow Mr. Magill went up and got his ribbon and prize money.

"This is it." Leeanne closed her eyes and wished she could close her ears too. She so wanted Gabe to win. He'd have gotten such a kick out of it.

"Our grand prize winner is . . ." the director hesitated slightly, "Gabriel Mendoza for his painting 'Blackbird and City Scene.' Accepting the award on behalf of Mr. Mendoza is Leeanne Mc-Nab."

A huge cheer went up. Obviously all of Gabe's friends had packed the place. In a daze, Leeanne hurried up to the director, took the ribbon, and the envelope containing the check.

Nathan hugged her, her parents hugged her, Mrs. Drake, Polly, and Mrs. Thomas hugged her too. But all she could think was that she wished Gabe was here so she could be hugging him.

"What are you going to do with the money?" Nathan asked as he pulled up in front of her house later that night.

"Oh, I don't know." It suddenly occurred to her she had to do something with the money. She couldn't keep it for herself. It wouldn't be right. "I'm going to give it to Lavender House."

Nathan grinned. "Good. He'd have liked that." He pulled her close and kissed her good night. Leeanne sighed in contentment. She still missed Gabe fiercely, but she had Nathan and the pain was getting better. "I think so too," she said, burying her face against his chest. "I think he'd have liked that a lot."

The exhilaration of the day had drained her energy. She was bone weary as she got ready for bed. Turning off the lights, she climbed between the sheets, closed her eyes, and drifted off to sleep.

She was awakened in the middle of the night by the loud song of a night bird. "Huh," she muttered groggily, "what's going on?"

Outside her window, the birds continued to sing.

"Night birds," she murmured, sitting straight up in bed. In the darkness she listened to the lovely song of the birds. She didn't know what kind of birds they were and she knew they weren't supposed to be here. It was the dead of winter.

Night birds sang in the spring and fall.

But they were singing their heads off. Loudly and clearly.

"Remember me when the night birds sing," Gabriel had said.

The bittersweet words echoed softly in her mind. The night birds were singing and she would remember him.

She lay there in the dark, listening to the birds and letting the images come. Gabe, lying on his bed with a teasing grin on his face. Gabe, his expression animated and his hands fluttering wildly as they argued about books. Gabe, feeding the birds to the music of Mozart as the hot Santa Ana winds whipped around them.

But Gabe was gone.

She wished with one part of her that she was imaginative enough to sense his presence. Only he wasn't there. His spirit was at rest and his soul at peace. He was gone.

And all she had left were the memories.

Leeanne took the check to Lavender House the next day. Mrs. Drake was delirious with happiness. "I can't tell you how much this means to us," she said, giving Leeanne a hug. She turned and hugged Nathan too. "Gabe would have been so pleased. What are you going to do with the paintings?"

"Well, I don't know," Leeanne admitted. "I'm definitely going to keep one of them."

"You could give us one," Mrs. Drake said. "These old walls could use a little life. Gabriel touched a lot of us, you know."

"Do you really want one?" Leeanne asked.

"Of course. Gabriel's work was exquisite. We'd love to have that one he painted of the park."

Leeanne looked at Nathan. He grinned. "Oh, go ahead," he said, putting his arm around her shoulders. "You know darned good and well that's exactly what Gabe would have wanted you to do with it."

"All right." Leeanne smiled as a great sense of rightness washed through her. "It's all yours. Just be sure and tell anyone who asks the name of the artist."

"Why don't I bring it by tomorrow on my way to work," Nathan suggested to Mrs. Drake. "That way I can help you hang it."

On the way back to Leeanne's house, she told Nathan about the night birds singing. He didn't say much except that sometimes the universe sent us messages in strange ways. She wasn't going to argue with that. She felt the same way herself.

There was an expensive car parked in front of her house. "I wonder who that belongs to," she said, glancing at the late-model Cadillac as she and Nathan went up the walkway.

They heard voices when they stepped inside.

"Leeanne," her father called, "there's someone here to see you."

Curious, she and Nathan hurried toward the living room. A tall, gray-haired man wearing an elegantly tailored suit was sitting on the couch. He rose to his feet.

"Leeanne, this is Mr. Brashire. He's the director of the Palladrino Art Museum," her mother said.

"How do you do," Leeanne said politely. She introduced him to Nathan.

"You're probably wondering why I'm here," Mr. Brashire said as soon as they were all seated.

"Well, yes."

"I'm very interested in your painting, Miss McNab," he said. "The one that won the grand prize in the art show yesterday."

"You mean Gabriel's painting," she corrected automatically.

"The artist, of course," he said smoothly. "But you are the legal owner, is that correct?"

"True." She wondered what he was leading to. "I'm the legal owner, but it's Gabe's painting."

"The artist died a few months ago," Nathan interjected. "He and Leeanne were good friends."

"I see." Mr. Brashire smiled. "I understand he left you three paintings and a number of drawings."

"Yes, but I've already given one of the paintings away," Leeanne said. "To Lavender House. That's the hospice where Gabriel died."

Mr. Brashire's face fell in disappointment. "I see. Would you consider selling the other two?" he asked hopefully.

Stunned, she stared at him. "Selling?"

"Yes. The artist was enormously talented." Mr. Brashire continued, "We'd like to exhibit his work. The Palladrino isn't world famous. Actually we're quite small. We showcase a number of local artists and craftspeople. We've not a huge acquisition budget, but I think we can come up with the money to buy Mr. Mendoza's work. We do have a fine collection."

Exhibit? Everyone would see his work. Everyone would see his name? He'd be remembered not just

for his remarkable character but for his art. Leeanne couldn't believe it. It was a miracle.

Gabe was right. Miracles did happen every day.

"You can have the one that won the art show,"
she began.

"Have?" Mr. Brashire queried. "You mean you'll
donate it to us?"

"That's exactly what I mean. But you can't have
the second one, I'm keeping it."

Mr. Brashire looked astounded. "That's very
kind of you, Miss McNab," he said. "Very generous. Do you think I could at least see the one
you're going to keep."

"Sure, I'll show it to you," she got up and started
for the door. "But it's not for sale at any price."

A few moments later she returned with the
painting of herself. Blushing, she held it up for Mr.
Brashire.

He studied it closely, a look of absorption on his
face. "Did you pose for this?"

"No, Gabe painted it from memory."

"I can see why you want to keep it," Mr.
Brashire sighed. "But if you ever do decide to put
it on the market, do please call me. This is a rather
superb work."

They made arrangements to get the painting to
the museum and Mr. Brashire left. Leeanne's parents disappeared into the kitchen to fix dinner.

"So how do you feel?" Nathan asked. He pulled
Leeanne down next to him onto the couch.

"I feel like it's over," she said thoughtfully. "Not
that I'll ever forget him, that's not what I'm trying

to say. I guess I feel like I've done what I can . . . oh, heck, you know what I mean. I loved him. But he's gone. The best I can do is make sure we remember him. I guess it sorta feels like I've done that. People will see his paintings and well, you and I will never forget him."

He leaned over and kissed her on the forehead. "I know what you mean. You've done what he wanted. But there's one thing you haven't done. One thing I know he would have wanted you to do more than anything."

"I know," she said. And she did know. "I've got to get on with my life. He's gone. I realized that last night when I heard the birds singing. Gabe wasn't there in spirit. No matter how much I wanted him to be, he was gone. He'll live in my heart forever and I'll never forget him but I've got to let him go."

"I think," Nathan said slowly, "that you already have."

January 24

Dear Diary,

Nathan and I took flowers to Gabe's grave today. It's been a long three months since he died and I've gone through a lot of changes. I guess I've learned a lot, who knows? All I know for sure is that life doesn't come with any guarantees. You do the best you can and you keep on going. Gabe changed me, that's for sure. Without him, I'd have never heard the night birds sing, never seen the neon in the rain, never listened to Mozart in the hot desert winds. I loved him. I guess that's the other thing I learned. That love doesn't come with labels or instructions; it just is. It sneaks up on you and takes a piece of your heart when you least expect it. Do I love Nathan? Probably. I can't imagine doing without him. Is it the same as what I felt for Gabe? No. It's different. But it's just as real. Anyway, I don't know what the future holds. Maybe Nathan and I will be together for the rest of our lives. Maybe not. Whatever happens, I'm not scared anymore. I guess that's the last thing I learned from Gabe. I don't let worrying about tomorrow steal the joy from today. Today may be all that we have.

Dear Diary

_Remember Me

by Cheryl Lanham
0-425-15194-8/$3.99

Leeanne never thought she'd love working at the hospice so much...or that it would be so hard. Her new friend Gabriel isn't like other boys. He is dying. But in his final days, he has one last lesson to teach her....

_Runaway

by Cheryl Zach
0-425-15047-X/$3.99

Cassie and Seth are in love. But when Cassie becomes pregnant, Cassie's father sends her to a home for unwed mothers and forbids her from seeing Seth again. Forced to choose between her family and the love of her life, Cassie begins to think of a drastic solution: running away.

—Coming in May 1996—
Family Secrets
by Cheryl Zach